I0819882

Also Available From Jacy Morris

Fiction:

The Abbey

The Cult of the Skull (The Enemies of our Ancestors: Book 2)

The Drop

The Enemies of Our Ancestors

Killing the Cult

The Lady That Stayed

The Pied Piper of Hamelin

This Rotten World

This Rotten World: Let It Burn

This Rotten World: No More Heroes

This Rotten World: Winter of Blood (Coming Soon)

An Unorthodox Cure

Movies:

All Hell Breaks Loose

The Cemetery People (Coming Soon)

An Unorthodox Cure

By Jacy Morris

FOREWORD

I've lost several people I love to cancer. Most people will experience the same pain if they live long enough. A few years ago, when my mom passed away from complications with cancer, I went through all the classic stages of grief: denial, anger, bargaining, depression, and acceptance. It was during the bargaining stage that I came up with the idea for this story.

What wouldn't I do to bring my mother back or to have saved her life? The answer is nothing. There's nothing I wouldn't do. And while this story is couched as a typical horror story, I hope it helps you the way it helped me. Developing this story helped me move through the stages and arrive at acceptance eventually. There's still a shitload of anger and occasional depression, but for the most part, I have accepted the loss of my mother.

This story was first created as a screenplay, and there is currently a movie in development of that screenplay, fingers-crossed. I have no control over the movie, and the script that I created has been re-written. The producers took something personal to me, an outpouring of my pain and sorrow, and handed it to someone else to re-write. I'm ok with that because it's going to put some money in the bank and some food on the table… like a good amount of food. There's going to be nachos. But, I wrote the novel because this story is personal to me, and I wanted people to see the meat and bones of what the story is supposed to be, and not the amped-up Hollywood version. I'll let readers and cinephiles decide which they like better.

From pain, often comes the desire to fix what is wrong. I am no different in this respect. If I could end cancer, I would, and with that in mind, I'd like to let you know that with each purchase of this book, I will be donating $1 to the Cancer Research Institute. So, if you bought the book, let me extend my heartfelt thanks to you. And hey, even if you hate it, at least you did some good.

Thanks for reading,
-Jacy

Prologue: In the Void

Silkerlax floated in a blue that was so deep and dark that it could be mistaken for blackness. The spaces between hung heavy and infinite, dulling the being's senses. The things it saw were not real; they weren't really there, but they were as well, shadows and flashes in the blue void, here one second and then gone another. Were they conjured up by its own mind? Or did the void predict the bent of Silkerlax's thoughts a split-second before it even had them, and then project them into the blue darkness? The flashes came so fast that, at first, the being hadn't been sure it had been seeing anything at all. But over the years, the thousands of years, Silkerlax had come to know them as reality.

Others floated in the void as well, as far apart from each other as one planet was to another. Somehow, the inky blueness let Silkerlax know about the presence of the others, their movements and torments echoing across the vast emptiness between. The being had spent millennia trying to reach its nearest neighbor, subtle waves of energy calling out and mocking its loneliness. Eventually, Silkerlax had given up. The prison would not let them be near each other; it would not let them plot and plan. And though Silkerlax had no love for the others, it found itself draped in a soul-eating loneliness as the frozen waste of the void stripped it of its flesh only for it to regenerate and begin the cycle again.

The being blamed The Pact. Oh, it was so long ago, The Pact.

It had been alive once, a being born to a mother, but forgotten as soon as its body touched the earth. It had been free to do what it wanted, to live, to hunt, to look up at the stars. Then came the boom, the sprawl of mankind, pushing it and its kind out of the quiet spaces they inhabited. The being and the others like him were forlorn, left to their own devices as the creator showed that it favored humanity more. And when they banded together to fight for what was theirs, the world that had belonged to them first, the creator had sided with mankind. The two races clashed then, the creator giving tools to the men and women, rituals that burned and seared the flesh of Silkerlax's kind. Its kind were more powerful than the humans, but their numbers were finite. It seemed to Silkerlax that in the time it took to kill one human, to possess its soul and crush it, another five humans had been born. It was a fight they could not win, but they couldn't lose either. The creator's agents brought them to the table, and they were forced to sign The Pact or be destroyed forever.

Silkerlax had never signed it. It had never agreed to The Pact. Few of his kind had. They had been betrayed, in the end, by the one who wanted to rule all, the one who wanted to be exempt from the rules of The Pact. So, the traitor signed under the guise that he was their champion, their spokesman, and before the blood had dried, they had found themselves in the void, the traitor nowhere to be seen.

The creator, Silkerlax scoffed for the millionth time. The demon thought it had an understanding of the creator now. Silkerlax had certainly had enough time to ponder the great being in the void. The creator would have never destroyed them. It needed them, for through them, the creator gained power, feeding off their belief in the creator's existence.

The deaths of the humans, in great swathes, was the reason the creator had become embroiled in the dispute to begin with. As the man things grew and spread, Silkerlax's kind toyed with them, made them kill the ones they loved and other fantastically brutal acts of depravity besides. Their goal had been total destruction, reclamation of the land that had once belonged to them. Reclamation of the creator's faith.

But the creator hadn't allowed it to happen, and the traitor signed The Pact, speaking for all of them. They should have held out for a world of their own, but the creator had always had a dark sense of humor.

Hate and longing built inside the being as its thoughts whirred in the same cycle for the billionth time. Silkerlax cycled through its favorite thoughts. It thought about the way the world was before, the way the world had been, the time of strife, and The Pact, and then Silkerlax ended the cycle by circling back around to thinking about its long imprisonment.

It had been so long. The Pact had diminished their presence on earth, but there was still a way to get free. The being longed for it, longed for the day when it would be called forth, when it would be allowed to taste freedom once again. And when the being did get free, when it was loosed from the chains foisted upon it, then The Pact would not enter into his mind. The being's only consideration, its only desire, would be revenge, pain and suffering, and freeing its brethren from their prison. Let the creator come to the bargaining table then. Let the creator try and make a deal with Silkerlax. All it needed now was the chance.

Then, as if merely thinking about it had brought it into being, Silkerlax sensed a shift in the void, subtle like the small shift in the morning forest when the darkness morphed into barely perceptible shadows. The light grew, and the being felt blinded. It recognized that light, though it hadn't seen it for millenia. The light sickened Silkerlax,

The light grew, and Silkerlax sensed the others that floated in the void. It sensed them coming closer, hurtling towards the light, closing the great distance that existed between them, but Silkerlax was the closest. It drove towards the light, a combination of red and white, blinding, and it understood. This was its chance. It would have a chance to take its revenge. It would have a chance to open the door wide.

It drove itself hard and fast, leaving behind some of its essence in its haste. The light swirled around it, and Silkerlax heard the screams of the others as it plunged into the light. It felt pain, joy, and love, and it knew it was somewhere different.

Diminished, Silkerlax waited, building its strength, waiting for its lost essence to regenerate. Somewhere, in a place unidentifiable, a part of itself grew, far away, keeping it connected to the void. It wasn't free. Not yet.

It heard sounds, speech, laughter, the grating sound of human voices. When the voices stopped and the new world went quiet, it explored its new prison, soft and fleshy, and it opened the prison's eyes. It saw a room. It saw the blinding light of the night through a window. Silkerlax forced a hand to raise into the air, and it beheld a wrist, delicate and small. It scanned the internal environs of its prison, and a name appeared, the name of its prison… Katie.

Silkerlax smiled, and then it reminded itself not to even think of its name, for its name was its undoing. It closed Katie's eyes and rested.

Chapter 1: The Bad News

Maddie Cutter lay on her bed... well, it wasn't her bed, but she felt like it was. She had been here enough times. *It wasn't the cancer that killed you; it was the treatment,* she mused. She could almost believe it. She had seen that line on one of her friend's Instagram posts. She hadn't seen that friend in so long, months. No one wanted to spend the night when your hair was falling out.

For months, she had undergone chemotherapy to treat a strain of acute myeloid leukemia. It was called acute because it was fast growing, but Maddie found nothing cute about it - *badum-CHING.* They called it a myeloid leukemia because the cancer had started in her bone marrow, then filtered down into her blood, and now it was currently infiltrating every organ in her body.

She turned her head to her left and saw her mother and father standing and talking to Doctor Wong. She liked Doctor Wong. Maddie thought Doctor Wong's job must be the most difficult job in the world. Despite the fact that Doctor Wong had to tell families every day that their child was going to die, the good doctor somehow managed to keep a smile on her face... well, for the most part. Right now, she wasn't smiling, and neither were her parents.

Maddie, with an arm that weighed a thousand pounds, reached up and ran a hand over her mostly bare scalp. She had managed to hold onto a few strands of hair, but she thought those few pathetic strands made her look even sicker. If she had been completely bald, she could have pretended she had chosen to look like a bowling ball. Her body ached. It wouldn't be long now though. That's what the look on her parents' faces told her. That's what the look on Doctor Wong's face said as well. The end was coming.

She sighed. It was a deep sigh, and as she exhaled, a part of her went with it, that part that she had been clinging to for so long, the part that kept saying, "Fight, Maddie. You don't want to let them down. You got this." She thought maybe she would have given up a long time ago if it weren't for her family and friends. Though many of her friends had stopped coming around, she still remembered their efforts to cheer her up after her first few rounds of chemo. But she had been sick for so long... her teenage friends could only maintain their sympathy and their worry for so long. Maddie didn't blame them. She had been like them once, silently crossing her fingers when someone became ill or turning the other way when she saw the suffering of the homeless in the streets.

As her hair fell out and the chemo continued, she shed friends in the same way that she had shed weight from her treatments. Now her friends only lived on her phone, healthy faces smiling and encouraging, but happy to have the ordeal end when they turned their phones off, happy to keep her and her suffering at arm's length. She didn't blame them. She wasn't supposed to be dying, but she was. Teenagers weren't equipped to deal with that suffering.

But now it would be over soon. Her father, mother, and her brother Clayton, could all get back to living something like a normal life. She wondered if they would preserve her room like a time capsule, the way parents sometimes did in the movies when one of their children died. Would her dad enter the room every now and then sit on the bed and cry? Would her mother pick up one of her shirts and smell it and do the same? How long until they stopped doing that? How long until they forgot about her and began to move on with their lives?

She didn't know any of these answers, and in truth, she thought it was unfair that she should even have to ask these questions, but she knew which way her arrow was pointing, and so she let it be. Her eyes felt heavy. She licked her dry and scabrous lips, and then she fell asleep to the hospital's lullaby, a combination of lightly beeping machines and whirring machinery.

****

Scott imagined that if he was ever going to pass out, this was the moment. A rush of blood ran through his head as his mind tried to make sense of the doctor's words. His knees wobbled like a newborn calf. He put his hands to his face, rubbing them across a day's stubble. His hands were rough and worn, a construction worker's hands. But all that toil, all those days on the construction site, he would do it all again, every day for the rest of his life if Doctor Wong would just take back the words that she had just uttered.

Scott pulled his hands from his face, not knowing what to do or say next. His wife, Angela, placed a comforting hand on his shoulder, and he wondered how she could find the strength to comfort him at this time, when he himself was too devastated to even say a word. Tears rolled down his cheeks, and he reached up and squeezed Angie's hand.

For a moment, he made eye contact with Angie. Her hair was wild. Her eyes were ringed with circles, mirrored by his own, brought on by months of sleepless nights and tears. She stood strong and true, and he envied her strength.

Doctor Wong continued her speech. It was one she had been forced to speak a hundred times to a hundred different families. It was never an easy speech, even after so much practice. "The cancer has metastasized. Right now, it's reproducing at a rate that we can't stop. I wish I had better news for you."

Scott heard the doctor, but he didn't want to believe it. He heard his own voice in his ears, panicked and weak, and he hated himself. "So what can we do?"

Angela looked at the doctor, waiting for a miracle to tumble from her lips, waiting for something that would give her, her husband, and her beautiful daughter some sort of hope.

"To be honest, Maddie's health is not going to get better. We can keep aggressively treating the cancer with chemo and hope that something different happens, but, in all likelihood, it's not going to help. The cancer is just too advanced. It's in more than just her bones and blood now." Doctor Wong stood there, the news broken, waiting to be of assistance. That was all she could do now.

"So what? We just give up?" Angela asked incredulously. There was a fire in her voice that sparked something in Scott.

Doctor Wong, somewhat defensively, replied, "I'm not saying that at all.

"Then what are you saying?" Angela asked.

Doctor Wong dropped her clipboard to her side, and she turned off the professional, almost formulaic persona that she had developed for times like this. She knew Scott, she knew Angela, had known them for a year of expensive, hopeless cancer treatment. They deserved more. "I know this is difficult–"

Scott interrupted, "I don't think you do know." Once again, he despised the weakness in his voice. He wanted to answer with the fire and veracity of Angela, but it wasn't in him. His words came out as a sob with syllables.

Doctor Wong continued, unperturbed. "–You're right. I don't know. But that doesn't change the reality that you have some real decisions that you have to make here." Doctor Wong watched the fight drain from Scott and Angela. She watched it fall from them, and she was careful not to take a step towards them, because she couldn't bear to crush what remained of that fight. "I know you guys are tapped financially. And I know how much of a hardship

Maddie's treatments are, and I'm telling you they're not going to cure her."

Angela and Scott turned their heads as one to regard their little girl. Through the window, they saw her, what she could have been, what she was going to be, but most of all what she was then, a wasted shell... a dying little girl. Doctor Wong's voice droned on, "We can work with hospice to make Maddie as comfortable as possible, give her some medication to take the pain away and make her time, when it comes, a little more bearable. But her time is coming, though no one here wants to admit it."

Maddie's eyes opened for a brief moment, brown eyes, so dark they almost looked black. No one mentioned that when they talked about chemo. No one mentioned how it drained everything, even the life in one's eyes. Maddie gave her parents a small smile, and then, as if she didn't have the energy to fight the weight of her own eyelids, her eyes closed again.

Tears fell from Angela's eyes. Scott, doing the only thing he could, put an arm around her shoulder and squeezed her close to him. He could feel it in Angela, the acceptance, the loss. He wanted to put his other hand to his own chest and press there to see if his heart still beat because he felt like he had just had it ripped out. He noted the curls at the corners of Maddie's mouth, and wondered how she could still smile after everything she had gone through.

"Let's take her home," Angela said.

"Ok."

****

Scott drove through the rain-slicked streets of Portland, two white-knuckled hands gripping the steering wheel. After helping his frail daughter into the backseat of the car, a feeling of anger had overcome him, flowing through him until he had to resist the urge to punch his own car. He didn't want to feel anger at that moment. He didn't want to be gripping the wheel of the car like it was cancer itself and he could strangle it to death on the ride home. He thought he should be feeling sadness. He thought he should be on the verge of tears... but he wasn't. His jaw ached from holding back the scream that threatened to erupt from his lips. He could feel it in the back of his throat, primal. He thought that if he let it loose, he might shatter the car windows.

In the back seat, Angela rode with Maddie's head resting on her shoulder. A blue blanket, from when Maddie was just a little girl, was wrapped around her. She was always cold after the sessions. A knit cap covered her head and the few wisps of sickly hair that still clung stubbornly to her scalp.

He couldn't stop looking at her and his wife. Every few seconds or so, he would take his eyes off the road and glance at them in the rearview mirror. He just wanted to check on her, to check and see that she was still there. *It isn't right. It isn't right that she should be taken from us. Why her?* She was so still back there. Angela watched the countryside speed by through the car window, and for a second, Scott knew he had a heart again, because it leaped into the back of his throat riding an avalanche of fear. *Was this the moment that she slipped away? On the car ride back home?*

"How are my girls doing back there?" he asked. His heart skipped a beat as Maddie's eyes opened, just barely. He pinched his lips to hold back the "Thank God" that crawled unbidden up the back of his throat.

"We're all fine back here," Angela said, making eye contact with him through the rearview mirror. She smiled, a strained smile, but it was meant for him. She could read him like a book, always could.

"When am I going to die?" Maddie asked.

Scott didn't know what to say, and he waited for Angela to take the lead, his mouth opening and closing, trying out words before actually speaking them. Angela was better at this type of stuff. If someone physically attacked his daughter, he would know what to do. He would beat the life out of them. If something needed to get fixed or repaired, he could do it. If Maddie needed to make a birdhouse for a school project, he could help her with that. But that question... *When am I going to die?* He had no answer for that. He had no fatherly wisdom that could put that question to sleep. All he had was the truth, and he couldn't even say it out loud.

All these thoughts took perhaps a second, a single beat of the heart, and then Angela said, "No one said you are going to die." Her voice was warm, reassuring, and for just a moment, even Scott believed her.

"Yeah, what are you talking about, kiddo?" He tried to match the tones of Angela's voice, tried to capture that nonchalant assuredness, but he knew his own voice rang false.

Maddie called him on it. If there was one other person that could read him like a book in this world, it was his own daughter. "You don't have to lie, Daddy."

The anger fled from him, and the sadness was there again, sadness at what he would be losing. Such a sweet little girl, everything a father could want in a daughter. *You don't have to lie, Daddy.* She just wanted him to know that she was ok. Even here, with the end in sight, she was looking out for him.

"Did you overhear what Doctor Wong said, sweetie?" Angela asked. Scott saw her rub the top of Maddie's head affectionately through the rearview mirror, and his daughter and his wife gazed into each other's eyes. He saw his daughter shake her head no.

"I didn't need to. I saw the look on your faces when you were talking. That's when I knew."

Poker. That's what his daughter would have been excellent at if she were going to lead a full life. Instead of watching her die of cancer, he should be sitting around the kitchen table with some boys from work, a couple of beers and a couple of root beers for the kid, teaching her the art of poker.

In the rearview mirror, he watched his wife go wordless. She leaned forward and kissed Maddie on the forehead.

"So when am I going to die?" Maddie asked, in such a cheery voice that Scott imagined that maybe there was nothing wrong with her at all.

Scott's eyes filled with tears, and the memory of anger was all but gone now. He pulled the car to the side of the road, swerving into a gravel parking lot, lest he drive off the road due to his blurry eyes. The car behind him honked, but he didn't care. He skidded the car to a stop, the wheels digging into the gravel on the shoulder of the road. With the engine still idling, he threw the car in park and unbuckled his seatbelt. He turned around and he made eye contact with his daughter. Her eyes were completely open now.

"Baby, we're not going to let you die," he said, and he felt it. The words felt real, and he almost believed them himself.

Maddie smiled at him. "It's ok, Daddy. Really it is. There's nothing you can do." Suddenly her smile turned into panic. She pawed at her mother with her hands, panic in her gestures. "Bag! Bag!"

His wife scrambled, pulling a plastic bag from the pocket on the rear of the front passenger seat. She handed the bag to Maddie just in time, and his daughter buried her face in the plastic, vomiting. The retches continued for some time, painful retching, their sounds making him wince in the driver's seat.

Scott sat contorted, facing the backseat. Maddie retched for so long that his back began to cramp up, and he was eventually forced to turn back around, his head hanging so that he couldn't see her suffering in the rearview mirror. The thought crossed his mind that he could just open the door and run away, never seeing his family again. In that scenario, he could always pretend... he could always pretend that his daughter had beaten cancer. He watched as the cars sped past, and finally the retching stopped.

"Don't worry, Daddy. I'm ready."

Still looking at the cars, he said the only thing that came to mind. "Well, I'm not." It was the truth, and it sang like it in the interior of the car. Angela placed a hand on his shoulder and squeezed.

Maddie continued speaking. Now that she had broached thc subjcct of her own death, it didn't seem so scary to her. "It's ok. I'll get to see Grandma and Grandpa Cutter. I'll watch out for you guys from above. Do you think everyone that ever lived is up there?"

Scott didn't know what awaited Maddie on the other side. He didn't care about the afterlife. He only cared about the here and now. "Yeah, I guess so," he said.

He put the car into drive and took a deep breath, readying himself for the road again. The sadness, the anger... they were all gone. Now he was just exhausted.

"Is there anything you want me to tell them when I see them?" Maddie asked.

It was a heavy question. A weighted question. To say anything would be to admit to Maddie that she was going to die. "Just tell them I love them, baby. Just tell them I love them."

Scott pulled back onto the road.

Chapter 2: Home

Angela breathed a sigh of relief as they pulled into the driveway. Maddie had nodded off once again, which she was thankful for. She was worried about Scott. He barely seemed to be holding it together. It was easier on Scott with Maddie asleep. He would bounce back. She knew that. He might be down in the dumps for a while, but he was a strong person.

In the meantime, she had to be the strong one, for everyone. She waited as he put the car into park.

Scott turned around to check on them. It was dark out, the interior of the car lit only by the flood lamp in their driveway.

"Shh," she warned. "She's asleep."

Scott opened his door quietly, stalking to the back of the car. Angela watched as he pulled the door open and gently unbuckled Maddie's seatbelt. Just like when she was a little girl, he pulled Maddie from the car, carrying her in his arms, her skinny legs dangling like the legs of a limp marionette. Angela climbed out of the car and rushed past Clayton's bicycle lying on the front lawn, a baseball card taped to the spokes to make it sound like, in her son's words, a "real motorcycle."

She reached the front door of their house, noting the quiet all around them, as if the world had stopped just for them, just to give Maddie some rest. She swung the door open and stepped inside.

She was greeted by the sight of her friend Gael rising from the couch. Though in her seventies, Gael was the most energetic woman that Angela knew. She was like a grandmother to her children. Her silver hair ringed her head in tight curls, and her smile was big and genuine. Large earrings dangled from her ears, and she put an aged finger to her lips as she walked towards Angela, a dancer's grace still alive in her legs.

Behind Gael, Angela saw Clayton asleep on the couch in his Iron Man-pajamas.

"Shhhh. He just fell asleep a few minutes ago." Her face went soft as Scott came in, nodding quietly to Gael. They watched as he turned sideways and ascended the stairs, Maddie's right arm dangling limply. When he was out of sight, Gael turned to Angela and whispered, "How'd it go?"

Angela can't find the words. She hasn't said it yet. She hasn't even admitted it to herself yet. She can't say the word "die," so she just shakes her head. "It's not good," she whispered, her voice dripping with the threat of tears. Finally, it was too much to take, and the tears broke the dam of her eyes and tumbled down her cheeks. Gael encircled Angela in her arms, and tears came to her own eyes. They embraced, sobbing quietly to avoid waking the children.

****

Scott soaked up the vision of Maddie's room, trying to etch every detail into his brain. The wall was covered in posters of bands he had never heard of. Her closet was full of clothes that no longer fit her because she had lost so much weight. On the mirror of her dresser, she had pictures of her friends, printed out from their plain, old computer printer. No one printed out pictures these days. How long had it been since Maddie had seen one of her friends? He couldn't blame them. They were just kids. Hell, he was an adult, and he was having trouble with it.

On her nightstand stood a lava lamp. Red orbs in golden liquid bobbed about, rising and falling as they gained and lost the heat emitted from the light bulb in the base of the lamp. The lava cast strange shadows on Maddie's face, and a shiver ran up his spine. She was asleep. Her stocking hat had come off her head, and he choked on a sob as he looked at the few scraps of scraggly hair clinging to her scalp.

He watched her chest like a hawk, never straying from the rising and falling of her chest for too long. He tilted a bottle of Bud Light up to his lips without even tasting the beer.

He heard her before he felt her, her hand on his shoulder... Angela.

"Come to bed," she said.

His eyes opened wide at the thought. He hadn't even considered the idea that he might need to sleep. If it wasn't for Angela, he might stand in Maddie's doorway for the rest of the night. "Did Gael go home?" he whispered.

His wife looked at him, concern on her face. "She left half an hour ago," she said. Scott could tell that his wife thought this was something he should have known, something that he should have been aware of. Maybe he should have, but he felt locked into something... something that he couldn't explain. It was like he was floating in the middle of a cloud. He could wave his hands in front of his face, see his palms, the calloused fingers from years of working with his hands... but he couldn't see anything else.

"Come on," Angie said. "Let's get some sleep."

He nodded at her, and she padded away. He let her get down the hall, and then he aimed one last glance at Maddie. He saw her chest rise and fall. He reached out and pulled the door closed. *I'll see you in the morning, kiddo.*

****

Angela pulled on a pair of gray sweatpants. Her mind wandered, flitting from thought to thought. She was trying to keep it together, she really was, but every so often, panic would rise up in her chest at the thought of losing her daughter, her Maddie. Maddie was her first child, and she had been everything they had ever wanted. She had turned out so perfect that they had then had Clayton as well. *Why not two perfect children instead of just one?* they had thought. Maybe they had been too greedy. Maybe this was God's punishment for striving for more. She shook her head as she tied the drawstring on her sweatpants.

They were baggier now than when she had bought them. With everything that had been going on she had often forgotten to take care of herself, going without food and sleep for nights on end. She needed to get better at that. She needed to be stronger.

Scott entered the room, plodding, his shoulders slumped. She looked at him, wondering what was going on in that great brooding brain of his. There was something to be said, but it would remain to be seen if he would actually say it. You couldn't force Scott to talk. He had to come to it on his own. Sometimes this would take days of brooding, sometimes hours, but eventually, he would burst like a summer thunderhead. Most of the time his worries were nothing, just an overactive imagination spinning petty concerns into great cosmic tragedies... but this time, it was a great cosmic tragedy they were dealing with, long and drawn out.

Angela pulled back the covers and climbed into the bed. She felt it calling her, as if her consciousness had already seeped from her body and was lying on the sheets beckoning her. She watched with lidded eyes as Scott peeled his shirt off. She liked the look of his back. It was soft now, but when they had been younger, it had rippled with muscles built from working on construction sites. He didn't do so much with his hands now. He had a good job, and people under him who were supposed to do all of the heavy lifting, but he was never one to let others do all the work. The muscles were still there, still defined, still attractive, but now they were under a layer of softness. She liked that softness.

Scott looked over his shoulder at her, as if he had felt her watching. "It's not fair, you know."

Here it came. The lightning before the thunder. "I know," she said. It wasn't fair. Not one bit.

He could barely make eye contact with her as he spoke, as if speaking his pain were some sin, something that only the weak engaged in. "Why, out of all the wicked people on earth, is our sweet, innocent daughter the one that has to go through this?"

It was a question she had asked herself many times since the day that Maddie was diagnosed. "There's no answer I can give you that's going to make any of this better." She wanted to have that answer; she wanted to be able to comfort him. But the truth was that Maddie had never done anything remotely wrong. It was not the answer that Scott wanted to hear.

He turned from her then, breaking eye contact, standing and staring into the mirror on top of the dresser, his head turning from side to side as he examined himself. "Am I a good man?" he asked.

She wanted to laugh. She wanted to slap him upside the head for being an idiot. She thought she knew where he was going with the question, but she just wanted to make sure. "What do you mean?"

He chewed on the side of his lip, and then he broke eye contact with himself in the mirror, unable to even look at himself now. "I mean, do you think there's something I've done to bring this down upon us? Lord knows it's not that little girl's fault. She's never done nothin' but good."

Self-pity, lord, how she loathed self-pity. She sat up in bed, ready to tear him apart, only tempering her fire at the last second. "Where are you going with this?"

He looked at her sheepishly, as if he had said too much already, and then he sat on the edge of the bed, his shoulders bending in on themselves. He looked old all of a sudden, more tired than she had ever seen him. "I just can't help but feel like this is my fault... that somehow I brought this upon her."

"There's nothing in this world that anyone could do that would justify what's happening to our daughter. This isn't our fault. We're not responsible for this." Her words had more steel in them than she intended, but only because she felt the words, knew them to be true. Scott buried his head in his hands. She leaned forward and placed a hand on his shoulder. His skin was hot, feverish with guilt and worry. "But I'll tell you what we are responsible for."

He turned to her then, and she saw the tears in his eyes, and her heart melted for him. She could count on one hand the amount of times she had seen him cry. Their wedding, the births of their children, the deaths of their parents... maybe two hands. Each time was as shocking as the first, but this time those tears grabbed ahold of her. "Together, we're responsible for the greatest gift we've ever had. We're responsible for all of the wonderful moments we've had with that little angel in there. And you're responsible for being strong and being brave so that Maddie and I don't have to do it all by ourselves."

Scott looked at her, her words worming their way through his brain. He looked confused.

"We don't have much time left with her, and I don't want to spend it sitting around being sad or being pissed off at the world. I want to spend it being thankful. I want to spend it soaking up every moment of our darling little girl." She eyed his face to see if he understood her.

He wiped his eyes with the back of his arm, whisking the tears away. He nodded his head. "You're right. You're always right."

Angela smiled at him. "Now there's something that a wife loves to hear. Come on. Let's get some sleep."

Scott smiled, his grief held at bay for one more night. He climbed into bed, sliding underneath the covers. She rolled over on her side, closing her eyes once more. He reached over her, draping his strong arm over her body. She reached to turn off the light.

Chapter 3: The Visitor

Maddie sat in the kitchen, poking at the monstrosity on her plate. *What the fuck is this?* She knew all the swear words. You couldn't go to school and not learn them. She liked the way they sounded. She liked saying them under her breath when no one was listening. She had even toyed with trying one out in front of her mother. *A girl ought to have sworn in front of her parents at least once before she died*, she thought.

Her friend Rosita did it all the time. It was second nature to her and her entire family. Rosita's parents didn't seem to mind either. Her parents and older brothers swore just as much as Rosita did. Still, she knew her parents didn't like swearing. They thought it made people seem low-class. *It's hard enough being brown in this world without handing them the proof that you're low-class.* Those were the words from her father, but that didn't stop her dad from cussing up a storm when he whacked himself in the hand with a hammer. That didn't stop her Mom from saying all sorts of swear words whenever she messed up dinner. Maddie was old enough to do it... and honestly, though she knew her time on the earth might be short, she ought to get some sort of perk from her impending demise.

She eyed the thing on her plate yet again. It was supposed to be a pancake she thought. But it didn't look like any pancake that she had ever seen. It was a neon glob of something that was halfway between a cake and egg yolk. It didn't smell particularly appetizing either. She felt her face flush at what she was about to do.

Her mom was washing the dishes after making breakfast for her. Maddie had slept in. Her father and Clayton had been up for hours. They were outside now filling up the swimming pool. She could hear Clayton's squeals in the backyard now. She used to hate his voice, high-pitched, always too loud. But ever since she had been diagnosed with the big C, she had learned to appreciate it for what it was, the voice of her brother, her brother who would have to grow up with the memory of a sister he had never really known.

She was tumbling this thought around in her mind when her mom looked over her shoulder, eyeing the orange pancake on her plate. Maddie gave the pancake another poke, hoping that the discomfort of being poked would force the alien food to sprout legs and run up off her plate. Then mom would have to make her something else.

"You have to eat, Maddie," her mom said.

"What the fuck even is this?" she asked. And immediately she regretted it. It felt mean. It felt disrespectful. She didn't know how Rosita could stand it.

She didn't look directly at her mother, and her mother only paused a second before saying, "It's an acorn squash pancake, with a little bit of garlic. It's supposed to help you fight cancer, boost your immune system."

It's fucking nasty, Maddie thought, but she kept the words inside her head. She didn't think she would ever swear around her mother again. "I'm not hungry." She pushed the plate away from her and sat there thinking. She wished she had the energy to get up and storm off or to walk down the street to a restaurant, but the only thing she had the energy for was sitting there in her chair and staring at the nasty pancake.

The next thing she knew her mom's hand was on her forehead. "Are you feeling alright?" she asked.

I haven't felt alright for months, she almost said. "Yeah."

Her mom removed her hand from her forehead, a worried look on her face. "Well, you don't have a fever. Do you not like the pancake?"

"I don't want to eat this stuff anymore," Maddie said, trying to get her tone just right so that she didn't sound whiny or ungrateful. Her mom was just trying to do what was best for her after all.

She felt her mom's hand on her shoulder, but Maddie couldn't look her Mom in the eye as she spoke, "We have to do everything we can, honey. We have to keep fighting."

"I'm not giving up." Maddie didn't think that she would ever give up. Rest maybe, but never give up. "I just keep wondering if this will be my last meal. I don't want acorn squash pancakes to be my last meal." She shuddered at the thought. "If I'm going to die, I want real pancakes, sweet and fluffy, covered in maple syrup and drowning in butter." Her mouth watered at the prospect.

Her mom gave her a lighthearted, backhand slap on the shoulder as if she were being ridiculous. "Baby, this is not your last meal. You have plenty of time, but you have to keep your strength up if you want that time. Do you want that time?"

Maddie looked at her mom and said, "Every second I can get."

Her mom smiled down at her, her head framed by the sunshine pouring in the kitchen window behind her. "Then eat the pancake. You're not going to like them if they get cold."

"Temperature isn't the problem," Maddie said under her breath. She knew her mom heard the words, but Maddie didn't care. She looked down at the pancake. She imagined it was her cancer. She imagined that here was the thing that was slowly killing her and that all she had to do to beat the cancer was to eat it. She picked up her fork and stabbed the pancake. She shoveled a bite into her mouth, her mom standing by her side. *It's fucking gross.*

Her mom bent down and kissed her on the top of the head. Then she turned around and returned to the sink to finish washing the dishes.

Maddie continued choking down the pancake, despite the incessant urge to vomit.

****

The sun was warm, warmer than it had any right to be. It caused the water gushing from the hose to take on a magical glow. Waves of light splashed across Scott's face, and he fell back in his mind, taking refuge in memories. He was reminded of their last family vacation on the sandy shores of Hawaii. He remembered the smell of pork at the luau, the smile on Angie's and Maddie's faces as they tried to hula dance with the brown-skinned dancers. He remembered the joy as Clayton realized he was really good at doing the limbo. It was a perfect time... perhaps the last they would have together.

"Daddy," Clayton said, his squeaky, little boy voice, failing to cut through Scott's memories.

Scott's memories of Hawaii morphed into another vacation, this time at Disneyland. Maddie was just a hair too old to appreciate the place on the level that Clayton did, but still old enough to have a smile on her face most of the time. He remembered a fountain, its crystal-clear waters reflecting off of his family's faces, the bottom of the fountain glittering with coins and wishes. He should have thrown one in, but he had never been one to waste money. When you came from nothing, you tended to hold onto your pennies, but that one time, he should have tossed in a coin and wished for something, standing among the hundreds of smiling children and grown-ass adults in fuzzy costumes. But he hadn't had the need then. He had no cause to wish for the health of his family... but he should have done it anyway.

"Daddy," Clayton said, his voice amplified by the outrage of unmet needs.

All those coins, all those wishes, and he couldn't even spare a quarter for his little girl.

"Daddy!" Clayton yelled, the impatience of youth driving him to do something that he knew not to do.

Scott jumped, the world in his mind evaporating as reality crashed into him. The pool. Clayton. Clayton needed something. He had to remember to pay attention to Clayton, just as much as he did his daughter, though his time with his daughter was almost through. "Yeah? What is it, buddy?"

"Why is everybody so sad?" his son asked, the earnestness in his voice pulled at his heart. He owed him an answer, but he didn't need to know just yet. He was so little. He wasn't ready yet for the realities of death. He could spare him that knowledge for another day at least. "We're not sad, Clayton. We're just tired. It's been a long week."

Scott's answer fell on deaf ears. Clayton was drawn like a moth to a light to the wavering waters of the pool. "Is it ready yet?" he asked, his mind flitting to a new topic, his question already forgotten.

"Almost," Scott said, breathing a sigh of relief at the sudden change of topic.

Clayton looked at him with the idolization that only a son can give a father. "Can't you make it go any faster?"

Scott smiled. "Can't wait any longer, huh?"

"I'm tired of waiting!" his son shrilled.

His son laughed then, knowing what came next. He angled the hose, bathing Clayton in a splash of chilly water. Clayton screamed in a combination of joy, surprise, and shock. He ran around the pool, waving his hands at the stream of water. Out of the corner of his eye, Scott saw Angela watching him through the window. He turned to her, and they locked eyes. There were a thousand words in the gaze that they shared. She smiled at him, and he smiled right back. From inside, he heard the ring of the doorbell, a deep sonorous tone that always felt too solemn for their home. But it wasn't broken, so he had never fixed it. Angie broke eye contact with him, and disappeared from the kitchen window.

Scott looked down at his sodden son as the child pulled on his hand. "Launchpad, Daddy! Launchpad!"

Clayton reached his skinny arms into the air, begging to be picked up. Scott took a quick glance at the pool to make sure it was deep enough. It was, so he bent down and scooped Clayton into the air. He squealed with joy.

"Are you ready?" he asked.

"Yeah!" Clayton screamed.

"Get ready for blastoff in 3... 2... 1!" Scott threw Clayton in the air, and he arced in slow-motion toward the pool. For a moment, he was backlit against the early morning sun, like an angel in flight, and then he landed with a satisfying splash, spraying water all over Scott's jeans. Clayton came up spluttering, but before he had even caught his breath, he was screaming for Scott to do it again.

****

Angela placed the last plate in the dishwasher. She closed the door and when she stood up, she saw Scott spraying Clayton with the hose. She stopped and let herself enjoy the moment. So much to do, so little time, but she could do this. She could watch the loves of her life smile and laugh for a change. Scott saw her, and she remembered the good times for a moment, the times before Maddie's illness. It seemed to her as if her life was going to be a three-act play. Act One... everything before the sickness. Act two... the sickness. Act three... everything after the sickness.

Before her thoughts could wipe the smile from her face, the doorbell rang. She wiped her hands on a dishtowel and threw it on the counter, shooting a quick glance at Maddie to see if she was still eating. She was, so Angela walked through the kitchen and into the foyer, her eyes briefly sliding over the pictures on the wall, barely registering their smiling innocent faces. If only the faces in the pictures knew what was in store for them, they wouldn't be so carefree.

The sun reflected off of the wooden floors. She stepped across the foyer, trying to see past the glare and through the tiny, iron-latticed window set three-quarters of the way up the door. All she could make out was the back of a man in a sports jacket.

She reached out and pulled open the red door, still trying to figure out who could be standing on her front porch.

At the sound of the front door opening, the man on the porch turned, and Angela saw him clearly for the first time. He was young, younger than she expected based upon the sports jacket he wore. It was the type of jacket that an older man might wear, fashion passing him by on a river of time. It was ill-fitting and seemed to be the type of thing that a man would buy only if he knew absolutely nothing about dressing himself. The man's hair was an unruly mop of black curls. Perched on his nose were gold-rimmed spectacles that also seemed a little out of place. His face was young, probably only a few years removed from being covered in the acne of youth. His bottom lip looked too pink, too wet. Behind his glasses, two intelligent blue eyes peered at her. She had never seen this man in her life.

"Can I help you?" Angela asked, fully confused about why a man like him would be knocking on her door.

"I'm a scientist," he said, as if that explained it all. Then he lapsed into an awkward silence. There was a small pause as Angela waited for him to say more, but no further words escaped the pink, too-wet lips of the scientist.

"Ok..." she began, ready to call for her husband if he said anything crazy. Perhaps that look in his eyes, which she had mistaken for intelligence, was actually the feverish light of insanity.

The sound of her voice seemed to kickstart the scientist in some way. "I've come about your daughter." He spit the words out, as if they had been lodged in his throat for some time, and at the mention of her daughter, Angela's skin crawled. She couldn't say why... she just felt something wrong.

"What about my daughter?" she asked, unable to hide the edge of protectiveness that crept into her voice.

The man, boy really, adjusted his glasses and looked down at his shoes. Then the words tumbled out of his mouth, as if he had been rehearsing them for hours, holding onto them the way a storm cloud holds onto its rain until it's ready to burst. The words came out in a gush that made Angela's head spin. "I think I can cure her. It's a complicated process. Some might say revolutionary. This new technique I'm pioneering is..."

The words rode over her like floodwaters and she reached out for the only words that floated and seemed solid. "I'm sorry, did you say you might be able to save my daughter?"

He looked up then, his eyes boring directly into her with a fever that she didn't quite care for. "Yes. Now I'm going to need to run some baseline tests, nothing too invasive. I think I already have a good handle on her case."

Other than the words "cure" and "daughter," Angela didn't hear another word the stranger said. She knew she shouldn't, but she held those two words in her heart. "Would you excuse me a second?" she said before slamming the door in the boy's face.

On the other side of the door, the young man pulled his spectacles off his face and scratched absentmindedly at a speck of dirt on one of the lenses.

"Scoooottttt! Can you come in here?" Angela yelled.

The boy on the other side put his glasses back on and waited with his hands behind his back. *Well, that actually went really well,* he thought to himself.

****

Angela could hear her children playing in the backyard. After she had told Scott about the boy on the porch, they had ushered Maddie out to play with Clayton. Now the young man sat in their kitchen, holding a cup of coffee up to his lips, gingerly blowing on the surface of the dark liquid and sending ripples playing across its obsidian surface. She thought she was going to explode. Cure. Daughter. Those two words rattled around in her brain, and though she knew she shouldn't, she had allowed the tiniest spark of hope to blossom in her chest.

Steam fogged up the boy's glasses as he took a sip of coffee.

Her husband stood leaning on the counter, a beer sitting within reach. As the stranger took another sip of coffee, Scott took the opportunity to put the beer bottle to his lips. She could read him well. She knew the way he slouched against the counter indicated that he was trying to look like he wasn't about to go ballistic. When Scott was quiet and trying not to look like he was angry, that was when she worried. Her husband wasn't a violent man, but he also wasn't one to put up with any nonsense.

In the brief conversation they had in their backyard, she could tell that he thought the whole encounter was nonsense. Scott didn't believe in miracles. He didn't believe in anything that he couldn't hold, or see, or touch. She knew that the boy in front of her was one wrong comment from being tossed out on his ass, but just in case... just in case that glimmer of hope in her chest was justified, she hoped that Scott held it together long enough to see, long enough to find out if what this boy said was actually true. Cure. Daughter.

"Mmm... that's very good. Is that a Costa Rican blend?" the boy asked.

She winced inside, knowing the effect that the comment would have upon Scott. True to form, Scott said, "I'm not sure where the coffee came from. You said this had something to do with our daughter." Scott punctuated his words with a clenched jaw and another sip from his beer.

"Right," the boy said, setting his coffee cup down on the table, next to a plate that still held a half-eaten, acorn squash pancake. "My name is Liam Brewster. I'm a scientist with the university, and I believe I have a cure for your daughter Maddie."

Scott looked at Angela, and Angela returned the look. She could see the doubt in his eyes and guessed that her own eyes mirrored his. Hope and doubt, two sides of the same coin, warred within her.

"Which university?" she asked, knowing that if she didn't ask, Scott would, most likely in a manner that would make the boy defensive.

"Does it matter?" Liam asked back.

For Angela, that was the wrong fucking answer, and the doubt in her heart grew, dwarfing the hope. "Considering you're in my home and you know my daughter's name, yes. Yes, it does matter." She could see Scott's jaw flexing out of the corner of her eye. It looked as if he were trying to chew his own teeth into bits.

Liam's head cocked to the side, and he said, "I'm from Western University. You can look up my bio on the internet if you wish."

It sounded fishy to Angela, and apparently it did to Scott as well as he pressed him further. "That's it? Just a scientist."

Liam adjusted his glasses again, an unconscious habit. Angela wondered if he even knew how often he did it. When he spoke again, he sounded unsure, as if he didn't quite have the confidence or the experience to say what he really wanted to say. "Well, a medical scientist specifically. I spend most of my time in a lab, doing research, double-blind studies, evaluating data and margins of error. It's probably quite boring to you, but that's not why I am here. Like I said, I believe that I have discovered a way to cure your daughter."

There they were... those words. Cure and daughter. For a second, she had started to believe maybe she had dreamed the whole thing. Maybe she had made some sort of wishful error and let a magazine salesman into her house. But, no, he had said it again. She took a sip from her own cup of coffee, the words tumbling through her mind. She felt the spark in her chest grow, however little.

Scott spoke with an air of disbelief, "You can cure cancer?"

"I'm not a hundred-percent sure," Liam said. He held his hand into the air, and his fingers twiddled about as if he were doing some sort of calculations. "More like 83.5 percent sure." He held his fingers in the air again, doing math, "With a margin of error somewhere in the three-percent range."

He seemed so sure about his numbers, but that wasn't enough for Scott. A cloud of suspicion crossed his face. "If you can cure cancer, why haven't we heard about this cure in the news or something? Why aren't you famous?" Scott asked.

Liam bobbed his head, as if to say it was an apt question. "Well, the cure that I have devised is somewhat esoteric in nature. If I were to propose this technique to my colleagues or to a medical journal, it's quite likely that I would be blacklisted from the profession."

Alarm bells went off in Angela's head. "Is it dangerous?" she asked.

Liam pursed his lips before answering, "Well, only to the degree that all untested medical techniques are. I mean, there's not a lot of data, so there's always a chance that something unforeseen can happen."

"This all sounds very shady," Scott said. "Maybe we ought to call the university." Scott reached into his pocket for his cell phone, and that's when Liam jumped into action.

He held out his hand and screamed, "No!" Scott looked at Liam with one eyebrow arched, and Angela got the feeling that Scott had been laying a trap for the boy. He had known exactly what sort of reaction he would get from Liam by threatening to call the university.

Liam, seeming to realize how untrustworthy he looked and began to ramble. "It's just that what I'm doing is so... outside the realm of normal that you could cost me my career. But believe me, I wouldn't be here if I didn't think it would work." He paused and then continued in an almost pleading voice, "Mr. Cutter, I can give your daughter a second chance at life."

Scott's eyebrow went up again, and he was very quiet as Liam's words tumbled around in his head. She could see him warring with himself. Angela felt the same way. She was stunned, speechless, and she didn't even know what this mysterious cure was yet.

"A second chance," Scott muttered, more to himself than anyone else.

Liam continued, "Please, just give me some time with your daughter. Let me run some tests. Do you believe in demons?"

She felt the hope in her chest wither away. Demons. Daughter. Cure. Those words didn't add up. He had said "demons." Just like that, as if it were the most ordinary thing in the world. She looked at Scott, and she could see which way this conversation was going to go. He broke eye contact with her, took a sip of his beer, and thumped it on the counter. He leaned forward, all business, no nonsense, and stalked over to Liam. "Come on, pal. Let's go. Time to leave."

Liam adjusted his glasses and stood slowly as he said, "But you haven't even heard everything that I have to say."

Scott spun Liam around and put a hand on his back, guiding him roughly to the front door. Liam limped along, looking over his shoulder at Scott. The look on his face said plainly that he had no idea where he had gone wrong. "I've heard enough," Scott said. "Out, or I'm calling Western University and letting them know what you've been up to."

Liam's shoes, worn dress shoes that had seen better days, squeaked on the floor as Scott propelled him to the front door. With his free hand, Scott pulled open the door and shoved Liam out onto the porch, the boy's arms windmilling to keep his balance. Angela followed, not knowing what to do. Demons? Cure? Daughter?

She wanted to hear more, but Scott wasn't going to let that happen. Liam spun around a panicked look on his face. He reached into the pocket of his old man's sports jacket and pulled out a business card. "If you change your mind..." he began, but before he could finish, Scott snatched the card out of his fingers, ripped it half, and threw it on the porch.

Scott spoke with iron in his voice, "We're not going to change our minds. Coming here and getting our hopes up. You're sick." She had only heard that voice a couple of times in her long marriage, but she knew what it meant. Scott was on the verge of pummeling Liam Brewster. He was slow to anger, but when he did, he was terrifying. All thoughts of interceding on Liam's behalf fled from her mind.

Then Liam said the absolute wrong thing. "I'm not the one that's sick."

Angela saw her husband's eyes bulge with rage, as if even his eyes were ready to attack Liam right there on the porch. Liam saw the look as well. He hastily straightened his glasses and turned to leave without a word. Scott stood for a moment, watching him go, his hands gripping the edge of the doorway with a white-knuckle grip. Then he turned and stalked past her without a word, leaving the door wide open. She was sure she felt the heat of the steam escaping his ears as he passed her. He would go have a beer and then tinker around in the garage, organizing his tools for an hour or two, before she would see him again. But he would be alright.

She stepped up to close the door to their house, surprised to note that Scott had not left handprints pressed into the edge of the door the way he had been gripping it. Before she swung the door closed, she looked down and spied the two halves of Liam's business card. Cure. Daughter... demons. At that moment, she didn't know who was crazier, her or Liam Brewster. She stooped down and picked up the two halves of the business card. She didn't bother looking at them. Instead, she shoved them into the pockets of her jeans and closed the door.

Chapter 4: A Downward Spiral

The next few weeks were happy ones for the Cutter family. Maddie seemed to gain some of her strength back. Scott pushed to take everyone on a family trip to Disneyland. At night, he would whisper to Angela about how great it would be, taking everyone on a trip.

Angela continued looking after Maddie, though secretly, she wished she was still able to go to work. Everyone at the accounting firm knew her situation, and they had been great, totally accommodating. Still there were days where she missed the tedium of crunching numbers and sorting receipts, trying to decipher the chicken-scrawl of any number of clients. It was a calming thing, a way to lose one's self without ever having to actually go anywhere. At home, all she had was constant worry... constant stress.

Every time she would bring Maddie a snack or check on her, she was afraid to find her cold and lifeless on her bed. For the sake of her family, she was able to pretend that everything was going to be alright, delude herself some might say. She made Maddie whatever she wanted to eat, eschewing the health foods that the internet told her would help Maddie in her fight. She stopped scouring the internet for miracle cures, and a tacit acceptance crept into her bones. She hated it; she hated the fact that she was coming to grips with the loss of her daughter. But she really had no other choice.

Maddie spent her time doing normal things. She wasn't able to go to school. Her immune system was too compromised for that, but she did text on her phone a lot. To who, Angela didn't know.

Clayton ran around the house with more energy than Maddie had ever had. He was so energetic, so bubbly. Maddie had always been a quiet, well-behaved girl. She had seemed almost like an adult from the time she was five-years-old. Clayton though, he was like a rocket let loose in the house. She would follow after him, cleaning up his mess, only to find that in the time she had taken to clean up after him, he had created two more.

Her only breaks came when Gael visited. Gael was every bit a member of her family as Scott or the children. She was a lovely, wise old woman. Angela had met her at the accounting firm, where she had done her time up until a couple of years ago when Gael retired. She was always ready with a smile or a bit of wisdom. Even if she hadn't loved Gael like an older sister, the effect she had on Clayton would have been worth her presence.

There was something about Gael that calmed the boy down, slowed him, made him able to stop and take a deep breath. She wondered if she would ever be able to learn the trick of how Gael did it, but there was nothing specific that she could see. She just exuded an aura of familiarity and family. She was magic.

Gael's visits were her only breaks from worry. Angela supposed that Gael's aura extended to her as well. They would sit and talk, about one thing or another, a bottle of wine shared between them.

But those days were few and far between, blessed though they were. Her regular routine was one of worry, waiting, and watching. And as the days turned into weeks, Maddie began to sleep longer. Dark circles ringed her eyes, and she started to smile less.

It was happening, Angela knew. She could delude herself all she wanted, but somewhere in Maddie's body, cells were growing unchecked, causing problems that would eventually kill her. Maddie was dying in front of her every single day, and there was nothing she could do about it but smile and wait for it to happen.

****

Scott's bones ached with exhaustion. He had maybe pushed himself too much at the job site that day. He should have let the younger guys handle all of the heavy lifting. But he couldn't, because every time he wasn't doing something, thoughts of his daughter crept into his mind.

His biggest fear was that something would happen while he was at work. He needed to work. They needed the money, the health insurance. Bills didn't stop coming because your daughter got sick. But every day, before he left for work, he said a little prayer in the hopes that God would not take his daughter away from him while he was at the construction site. He didn't pray for a miracle, because it was clear that God was going to take her no matter what, but the way he saw it, the least the main upstairs could do was to let him be at home when it happened.

His arms ached from carrying bundles of sheeting and wood around, but he couldn't help himself. Working kept his mind off of home. Even then, he stopped to check his cell phone every ten minutes or so. Sometimes, when he was moving, he wouldn't hear or feel his cell phone go off.

He hated the stares from the guys on the site. They were sympathetic, worried. He had worked with most of the guys for years, had beers with them, been to their barbecues, births, and baptisms. But he didn't like what he saw on their faces anymore. He thought he saw pity. He would not be pitied. And so he applied himself even harder to the work, to bury those stares, to bury those thoughts.

When Scott got home, he was racked with guilt. While he was gone, Angie was home all day, keeping an eye on Maddie. She looked exhausted herself. He ought to do something, give her a break, but he knew if he brought it up, she would just deny it. She wouldn't be apart from Maddie. She couldn't make herself do that. It was another reason to feel guilt... because on the job site he could sometimes manage to forget, even if it was only for a couple of minutes.

He loved the sound of noise when he came home. It meant that everything was alright. He loved to hear the sounds of Angie cooking in the kitchen, Clayton's feet pounding through the house as he ran from one random spot to another, the sound of his daughter's voice in the living room, laughing at something on the TV. These were normal sounds. And, if no one came running to greet him, he thought that was alright because then he could stand in the foyer, just listening and pretending everything was going to be normal. Standing with a hand on the railing at the foot of the stairs, he could pretend that it was all going to be ok.

But when he stepped into the living room... he knew it was not going to be ok. He would see Maddie, bundled underneath a pile of blankets even though it was plenty warm out. He would see those rings under her eyes, the dryness of her lips as if she were incapable of moistening them on her own anymore. He would see that stocking cap on her head to hide the small amount of hair she had left, and there was no chance of pretending.

Even now, with Clayton in bed, and Maddie snoozing on the couch as the TV droned on and on, he couldn't forget. She had left it on the Cartoon Network before passing out. Maddie controlled the TV these days... it was a small price to pay for time with his daughter.

Angie sat next to him on the couch, her hand intertwined with his. They sat silently, watching their daughter, listening to her breathing. It wasn't as strong as it had once been. It was sort of raspy, as if she always had something stuck in her throat, and it was uneven, sometimes stopping altogether. Maybe it was just sleep apnea. Maybe... but he had never heard of a person so young having sleep apnea. But what did he know? He was just a construction worker.

As he was thinking about all the things he didn't know, she went through another of those long pauses.

Angela squeezed his hand so hard that he thought it would break, and they waited, holding their own breaths, waiting for some sign that Maddie was going to be alright. He could hear his own heart beating in his head. His ears grew red and hot from the fear that his daughter had just died, and only his grip on Angela's hand kept him from rising up off the couch and checking on his child.

Just when he thought he couldn't stand it anymore, her mouth opened a small bit, and a rattling breath entered her lungs. He could breathe then. Angela untangled her hand from his and placed it over her own mouth. She ran then, out of the living room, her eyes glistening. He wanted to call to her, but he didn't want to wake Maddie. Instead, he sat on the couch, oblivious to the childish cartoon on the TV. He watched her chest, looking for the rise and fall. He listened to her breathing, holding his own breath on every pause.

****

Angela fled to the kitchen. She always felt comfortable in the kitchen. It was a safe place, a place full of homey, comfortable smells. It was bright, all the shadows chased away by the bright lights above. She knew every inch of that kitchen, knew what was in each drawer, what food items were in the pantry. Hell, she knew how old the milk was in the fridge. The kitchen's familiarity comforted her.

It allowed her to think of happier times, moments she and her family had spent in the kitchen preparing meals, listening to the radio. It held everything she needed to distract herself from the truth. Maddie was dying.

She leaned forward and gripped the sink, her tears making tiny metallic clangs as they landed on the dry bottom of the sink. She wept silently, unwilling to wake up her daughter with her sobbing. When the storm had passed, she reached into the pocket of her jeans and pulled out two tiny bits of paper. She placed them on the bright wooden counter, arranging them and lining them up so that the torn halves interlocked, a two-piece jigsaw puzzle.

There were times during the day when somehow she would find herself staring at the card, licking her lips and clearing her throat as if she were about to pick up the phone and make a phone call. Then, she would take both halves of the card and stuff them back in her pocket. The business card was worn now, the edges fraying, but that didn't matter since she knew the number by heart. Angela recited the number over and over in her head. *If there's a chance... if there's even the smallest of chances, why shouldn't I call the number?* She had had the argument with herself many times over the last few weeks... and always her answer was one of fear. *What if he hurt her? What if he made her die faster?* She wasn't willing to take that chance... not yet. She pulled the torn halves of the business card toward her and stuffed them in the back pocket of her jeans. She looked out the dark window, trying to find answers in her own reflection, but none were forthcoming. *If there's a chance,* she began... but then she fought herself again. Eventually, she would go and sit on the couch once more, waiting and listening for Maddie's breaths beside Scott.

****

Father Romero, an old man, strong and tall, stood at the pulpit and looked out over the nave. They sat in pews, men, women, and children of every race and age. He was happy to see them. He was happy with the diversity in front of him. That he was able to reach people from every walk and station of life meant something to him. He knew some priests that could only reach those that were like themselves, and though he knew this was pride on his part, he believed a priest who couldn't reach everyone wasn't worth a hill of beans.

He tried to smile at his congregation, for he knew how severe his face looked, with his sunken cheeks and his square head decked with silver hair. He knew he could look like a furious corpse at times. But smiling helped.

"God's plan is not one that we can understand. Though we follow His word, it's trust and faith that we offer. Through trust and faith, all is made right. All is made the way that it is supposed to be. We may not like the plan, but this is the test that is set before us..."

Father Romero's eyes found the Cutters in their customary pew. He had chosen his words for them. He knew that they were struggling through a difficult time; he knew they would need his strength and the strength of the congregation. But most of all, he knew they would need the strength of God. For when tragedy struck, faith was tested. The sight of little Maddie Cutter leaning on her father almost took his breath away. She had been such a robust, healthy girl but a few months ago it seemed.

"... for we are humans. We were made in his image. But that's all that it is, folks. An image. A pale reflection of His glory and His greatness. It's up to us to keep the faith, to keep ourselves close to God, and to walk the path of righteousness. If you do that, then the plan will all make sense, and you will earn a spot next to Him for eternity. And what more could a person want?"

The priest wanted the Cutters to hear him. He wanted the Cutters to take solace in his words, to be comforted in this holy place. He wanted them to feel the embrace of God and know that what they were going through was terrible but that they weren't alone. He wanted all of these things, but he could only hold the branch out to them. They must be the ones to take it... for such was the nature of faith. You couldn't trick people into it. You couldn't buy it with false promises of miracles. Faith had to be given freely.

He nodded at Scott Cutter, hoping that the man had really heard him and his message. But there was no telling if this was the case based upon the hard look on the man's face.

"Before we leave today," Father Romero continued, I want to ask that you join me in sending up a prayer for our own Maddie Cutter. For though God has a plan, it never hurts to ask for a favor. Please, join me in a moment of silent prayer for Maddie."

He bowed his head, trusting that the congregation would do the same. They were a good congregation. He was a lucky man. There were a few rough edges in the crowd, but who had ever been perfect? Who had ever been without sin? No one that he knew, certainly. He said his words for Maddie, putting his heart behind them. Warmth filled his body, and he hoped that it spread to the Cutters. As he opened his eyes and raised his head, he saw the look on Scott Cutter's face. He stared straight ahead, chewing on his lower lip.

"Amen," Father Romero pronounced. The congregation echoed their own amen, and then the people rose. He saw the Cutters begin to rise, all except for Maddie. Scott picked her up in his arms, cradling her as if she were a five-year-old instead of a fourteen-year-old girl. Father Romero moved through his congregation, shaking hands with people and greeting them as expediently as possible. The priest moved quickly to where the Cutters were. He smiled as he approached, trying to not look like a walking mummy.

Scott, still holding Maddie in his arms, saw him first and almost grudgingly said, "Thank you for the kind words, Father."

"They're not just words, Scott. They're the truth."

"I guess we'll see," Scott said. Then he turned, maneuvering through the crowd, dodging knots of people standing and talking. Clayton followed after him, his small, black-haired head lost quickly among all the adults.

Father Romero felt a light touch on his elbow and jumped slightly. It was just Angela, a look of regret on her face. She said, "Don't mind him, Father. He's just in pain. We're all in a lot of pain."

"I understand," he said.

She just nodded.

He wanted to reach out and hug her. He wanted to wrap his arms around her and take her hurt away. He did understand. "The pain you're feeling is no less than that which I feel when any one of my congregation falls ill." She didn't answer him. She just offered a meek look of apology, and then she began making her way through thc thinning crowd, leaving him behind. He wondered if he had failed them. Before she was hidden from his sight, he called after her, "Let God be your salve, Angela Cutter." Then she was gone, and Father Romero stood in his church searching for a sign from God.

Then the rest of his congregation was upon him, pressing their hands to his, and telling him that he gave a wonderful service. But he didn't feel their words. He was too busy remembering the faces of Scott and Angela Cutter... and the wasted face of Maddie.

That night, as he tried to surrender himself to sleep, the priest tossed and turned with Maddie's face in his mind. Only after another round of prayers for the Cutters could he finally fall asleep.

****

Angela placed another plate on the dining room table. She preferred eating in the kitchen, with everyone spread out where they preferred to eat, but a part of her felt a duty to give Clayton the memory of sitting around the actual dining room table with his mother, father, and sister. She didn't know if he would remember such things. Four-year-old memories were such hit and miss affairs. She was still surprised by the memories that Maddie could recall from when she was young, a time when she fell in the street and scraped her knee when she had barely been three, being left in a living room at a party with people they were no longer friends with. She hoped these memories took for Clayton. She hoped he would remember Maddie's kindness to him. Maddie had never shown anything but love to Clayton. It would be tragic if he had no memory of her.

She placed the fourth plate on the table and pulled on the corner of the tablecloth to straighten a wrinkle. Scott sat on the couch reading a self-help book on his tablet. Try as she might, she could not get Scott interested in reading anything besides those damn self-help books. She didn't even bother asking him about what... it was all just common sense wrapped up in an extended metaphor. Scott didn't need self-help books, but he read them anyway.

As if on cue, Clayton came darting around the corner, his heels slamming against the hardwood floors of the dining room. The way he ran around here all day long, she could swear that someone was spiking his morning o.j. with speed. "Clayton! Go get your sister! It's time for dinner."

He skidded to a stop in his socks, his arms pinwheeling to maintain his balance. "What's for dinner?" he asked.

"Tuna casserole," she said, wondering if he had already forgotten that she had told him to go fetch his sister.

"Yuck," he said emphatically before he spun on the floor, his bony arms pumping as he charged up the stairs.

Angela followed the stomp of his feet overhead, imagining small piles of plaster dust sifting down from the ceiling. That boy was all heels. From his chair in the living room, she heard Scott call, "I hate to say it, but I'm in agreement."

She knew he was joking, but the comment irked her to the point where she brought out her imaginary scale. On one side was the part of her that needed to decide if she was going to explode balanced on the other side by the part of her that would let things slide. Though she had made dinner and cleaned the house and watched after the kids, the "let it slide" part of her scale dipped lower than the "explode" side. "You know, for two people that seem to hate tuna casserole, you both eat a surprising amount of it."

Without removing his eyes from his tablet, Scott said, "Yeah, well Clayton is a growing boy. You could put concrete dust in front of him and he would eat it."

"Uh-huh. And what's your excuse?"

"I'm too lazy to cook for myself."

Her scale wobbled back and forth. Did she lay into him because of his typical reinforcement of gender stereotypes, or did she let it slide? The scale balanced out, leaving it up to her to decide. "You're too lazy to do a lot for yourself. If I left you alone for a week, the police would find your corpse lying on the floor with that tablet in your hands, dead from starvation."

Scott was about to offer a rebuttal when he was interrupted by a terrible sound. "Mooooom! Come quick!" It was Clayton, screaming, urgency in his voice. Angela and Scott forgot their argument, an argument that had repeated itself a hundred times during the course of their marriage.

Scott leaped out of his chair, his tablet flying across the room. Angela felt her heart leap into the back of her throat. Then they were sprinting up the stairs to the second floor of the house. Clayton continued to scream for them, calling them, panic edging his voice. The floor vibrated with their steps.

Then they stood in Maddie's room. Angela's hand went to her mouth to stifle a sob of pure trepidation. She saw her little boy standing next to his sister's bed. Clayton still screamed. He knew Maddie was sick, and she wouldn't wake up, even though Clayton was shaking her as hard as he could. She could see the terror in his eyes, as if at that moment, he had just realized what death was.

She rushed into the room with Scott at her side.

"She won't wake up!" Clayton cried. She pulled him out of the way, hoping that maybe, just maybe, she was only sleeping deeply. Scott stepped up to the side of the bed and gripped Maddie's shoulders. "Maddie? Baby?"

"Why won't she wake up?" Clayton cried, snot running down his face. Angela didn't answer him. She didn't know if Maddie was dead or not. Then the words crawled out of her mouth like a slug with fishhooks sticking out of the sides. "Is she dead?"

Scott pressed a hand to Maddie's throat, feeling for a pulse. He turned to Angela and shook his head. A sigh of relief escaped her, and she turned to Clayton and said, "No, honey. She's just sleeping." Then she turned her son around and prodded him out of the room. He looked at her with doubt on his face as he passed the door's threshold. *He knows that something is wrong, but I don't have the time to tell him what it is.* "Mommy needs you to wait downstairs, Clayton."

She closed the door with him still looking at her, looking lost and forlorn in the hallway, and for the second time that night, she felt as if her heart was going to break. With the door closed, she rushed over to Maddie's bed. "Oh God, what is it?" she said, placing her hands upon Maddie's arm. "Wake up, Maddie," she begged. Then she pressed her hand to Maddie's throat to feel for a pulse. She needed to feel it. She needed to know that blood was rushing through her body, that her brain was being fed oxygen, that her baby was still there.

Scott shattered. Tears welled in his eyes reflecting the dull light of the lamp on the nightstand like shards of broken glass. "Maddie?" he asked softly. There was no response but the rise and fall of his daughter's chest. He thought that maybe he wasn't loud enough, so he shouted her name, scaring himself with the force of his own screams. He squeezed his eyes shut, and tears ran down his cheeks. "Wake up!" he commanded, anger vying with the sorrow growing in his chest. *Maybe she can't hear me.* He shook her, first gently, then violently.

Angela stepped back, not sure of what to do. She saw Scott losing it. She saw him falling apart. She put her hand to her head as if she could pull an answer from her brain that way. "I'm going to call an ambulance." She patted her pockets until she found her cell phone. She pulled it out and dialed the numbers with trembling fingers. She didn't know what to do. She had never had to call 911 before.

Scott stopped trying to wake Maddie. He sat on his haunches, clutching his little girl's hand in his own. He seemed to be trying to will her awake, but still Maddie didn't respond.

Somehow, Angela stumbled through the conversation on the phone. An ambulance was on the way. They waited, hoping that at any second Maddie would sit up and pretend it was all a joke. Not until they heard the sirens of the ambulance did Angela admit that something was seriously wrong with her daughter.

****

The hospital smell didn't bother Scott anymore. At first, he had associated it with death, with his little girl's sickness, but now he was glad of it. The clean, astringent smell meant that they were in a place where someone could help his daughter. The hospital was the only option he had for hope, and he desperately needed to know that this wasn't the end.

In his mind, Scott had always imagined that he would be able to say goodbye or at least share a hug with Maddie before she died. This... this... was a... travesty. He could think of no other word. "Travesty, travesty, travesty" was all that ran through his mind.

She lay in the bed, her eyes closed and the faint memory of a fairy tale princess filled in the small corners of his mind that currently weren't occupied with worrying about his daughter. She was a princess, just slumbering, and somehow the doctors would find a way to waken her, and they would all live happily ever after.

He avoided looking at Angela, keeping his eyes locked on Maddie in case she woke up. He didn't want to miss the moment if it happened. He was exhausted, his eyes felt like sandpaper, but he avoided looking at Angela because he didn't want to see what she looked like or see the echoes of his own exhaustion reflected in her face.

The doctor entered the room, but Scott didn't even spare her a glance. For Scott, the doctor was both welcome and unwelcome at the same time. Her hair was disheveled, and she looked as if she had been awake for hours. Her make-up-less face showed the strains of the evening upon her. Dark circles ringed her eyes, and her cheeks seemed to want to drip off her skull like a clock in a Salvador Dali painting.

Angela, impatient with waiting, asked, "Is this the end, doctor?"

The doctor's voice was grim. "I wish I had better news. It looks like Maddie's body is shutting down. She's in a coma."

Coma... coma... he had heard that word before in movies. Whenever someone went into a coma, they would miraculously awaken, just as good as new. "But will she wake up?" he asked, knowing that the movie versions of comas were probably more than a stone's throw away from the reality.

"I don't know," the doctor said. He could hear the sympathy in her voice, but he avoided looking at her face. He didn't want to see if she was lying. He didn't want to see her avoid eye contact when she spoke of his daughter. Scott would know what that meant. "If I had to put money on it, I would say no. It's just a matter of time."

Panic welled up in his chest. *This is happening.* "Isn't there something we can do? Do you know of any experimental drugs, any trials that we can get into? There must be something we haven't tried. There's got to be something."

Scott could see the hurt on the doctor's face, and he knew he was putting her in an unfair position, but at that moment he didn't really care. He had been in an unfair position for over a year now. The doctor shrugged her shoulders before speaking. "I wish I could give you some sort of hope, but it's just a waiting game now."

"So this is it?" Angela asked. Scott couldn't believe the defeat he heard in his wife's voice. He hung his head and squeezed Maddie's hand a little tighter. He didn't think it was right that a mother should carry defeat like that in her voice when it came to her own child.

"I'm afraid so," the doctor said. "We'll make her as comfortable as we can, but there's really not much we can do at this point."

Scott tried to focus on the steady beeping of the EKG rather than listening to the doctor. It was a good rhythm, a good heartbeat. Maddie couldn't be dying. This was not the heartbeat of someone that was dying.

Scott sensed that the doctor was done talking. He glanced at her for just a second, mentally dismissing her, and her clipboard dropped to her side. "I'll leave you alone," she said. "Just press the call button if you need anything."

Scott didn't hear the doctor leave. He was too engrossed in watching the peaks and valleys of Maddie's EKG. *They're mistaken. She'll wake up any moment now.*

He didn't even hear as Angela exited the hospital room. He had eyes and ears only for Maddie, as if holding her hand and keeping watch on her could keep death from creeping into the room and snatching his baby away. He refused to even blink until his eyes could stand the sting no longer.

****

Angela didn't know where she was going. She just needed to get out. She needed to escape from the room where her daughter was dying and her husband was falling apart. That Scott was falling apart couldn't have been more obvious. He didn't even say anything as she left.

She walked through the hospital, pointedly ignoring any open doors. She didn't want to see the pain inside those rooms, the suffering. She had her own pain and suffering to carry. Any more might force her to collapse to the ground where she'd never get up.

It was nighttime. The hallways were as quiet as they would ever be in a hospital. When she saw other patients in the hallway, Angela averted her eyes. She didn't want to be a part of their pain, and she didn't want anyone else being a part of hers. She stopped and stared at a bulletin board for a while, re-reading a poster about how to protect yourself from germs several times until she gave up. She didn't comprehend the pictures and the words. She couldn't stop looking at the cartoon drawing of a little girl washing her hands at a sink. The little cartoon girl looked like Maddie when she was that age.

She shuffled away when she found herself wondering if little cartoon girls contracted cancer. A sign pointing to the cafeteria caught her attention. People eating, maybe even laughing. That might take her mind off things for a moment.

As she stepped into the cafeteria, people avoided eye contact with her. No one looked up from their food. The cafeteria was not full, and it had the feel of a place that was shutting down for the night. The food cases, normally full of the day's dishes, were cleared out. A cafeteria worker wiped them down with the energetic bustle of one who was about to be free of work.

The tears in Angela's eyes clung, unfallen, lending the entire world a look as if it were underwater. She was not hungry. She wondered if she would ever be hungry again. She spied a couple of carafes of self-serve coffee and made her way over to them. She had to do something; she couldn't stand in the middle of the cafeteria like a zombie. Already people were turning to look at her. After fumbling with the cardboard cups, she depressed the button on the lid, filling the recycled cardboard cup with black liquid. The coffee had a slightly burnt smell to it, and she wondered how long ago it had been brewed. The old coffee suited her just fine. She managed to slip a cardboard sleeve onto the coffee cup just as her fingertips began to burn from the heat.

At the checkout, a disinterested worker rang Angela up and deposited her change in her hand. She shuffled to a table in the corner and sat with her hands around the coffee cup. *What am I doing? I should be by Maddie's side.* The thought bothered her, made her feel like a bad mother. Then she saw something... something that she knew had been there the whole time, calling to her. She had seen it once before, out of the corner of her eye during another long visit to the hospital, when Maddie had first undergone testing for cancer. That day Clayton had skipped breakfast. He had been too engrossed with building himself a fort out of couch cushions, blankets, and all the pillows in the house. A hungry Clayton was a terrible Clayton, so when the hunger hit him in the waiting room of the hospital, she had brought him down to the cafeteria and gotten him a hot dog. Somehow, she remembered the item's presence, though it had not been anything she was looking for at the time.

It seemed so alien, so out of place. She stood from the table slowly, her chair scraping against the tile floor. She knew though... she knew now why she had left Maddie's side. She sidled up to the payphone, perhaps one of the last in existence, and she set her coffee cup down on a counter. She fumbled in her pocket for the change the cashier had given her. She lifted the receiver, marveling at how heavy it was. It had been a while since she used a telephone with an actual cord on it. The quarters clinked into the reservoir somewhere deep in the payphone's innards. She dialed the number from memory. As the phone rang for the first time, she took a sip of coffee, slightly burning her tongue. The taste of burnt coffee filled her mouth.

On the second ring, someone picked up the phone. A voice said, "Hello?"

"It's me, Gael." She loved the sound of Gael's voice, warm, motherly. Angela would never tell her such. Gael took pride in the fact that she was still young, though technically she wasn't. She didn't like being reminded of the fact that she could be a grandmother, or a great grandmother for that fact.

Gael said, "Well, I'm glad I picked up. I didn't recognize the number."

Angela didn't know how to start. She didn't know how to break the news to Gael. Oh, sure, she probably already had some sort of clue considering that she was currently babysitting Clayton, but she couldn't say the words... she couldn't say... "Yeah, I left my phone at the house." That wasn't what she had meant to say. "I wasn't thinking straight."

"With all that you guys are going through, that's understandable, dear."

Is it? Angela wondered. *Is anything understandable anymore.* "I'm using a pay phone," she blurted, as if it was the most interesting thing in the world. "Can you still believe they have these things?" She fell quiet, and there was no answer from the other end of the line. Her mouth opened and closed. She knew what she had to say, but she didn't know how to say it, or she refused to say it, or she can't say it, or any of another dozen excuses.

"What is it, Angela?" Gael asked.

She knows. Gael already knows. Though she knew this to be true, she still couldn't say it... she can't say... it. "It's bad."

"How bad?" Gael asked, her voice warm with compassion.

Say it. "We're just... we're just waiting." There was a long pause. The sob that she had been fighting back escaped her. She put a hand to her mouth to stifle it. She could feel the few late-night denizens of the cafeteria eyeing her now, probably glad that they were at the hospital for something less grief-inducing.

"Do you want me to bring Clayton up there, so you can all be together?" Gael asked.

Oh, God. Clayton. The thought of her little boy staring at his comatose sister on her death bed filled her with fear. "No, let him sleep. He can come up tomorrow." *Maybe then, I will have prepared myself for the moment he sees her.*

"Do you need me to bring you anything?"

A miracle. "No. I just need my daughter back," she sobbed.

"She's still there, Angela. Don't forget that."

Angela nodded her head, though she knew that Gael couldn't see her. Even then, Gael probably knew she was nodding. She always seemed to know everything. Angela couldn't speak anymore. She was afraid that if she tried, she would start wailing into the receiver and not stop until someone dragged her away from the phone. She took a deep breath and said, "I'll see you in the morning, Gael."

"Call me if anything changes, or if there's anything I can do. I'll be there before you can even hang up the phone."

"I will, Gael. Thanks." *There. That sounded almost like her normal self.*

"Anything you need. Don't hesitate to call me. You're not alone."

But I feel alone. "I have to go." She hung up the phone and leaned against the wall, her eyes pinched shut, thoughts upon thoughts avalanching in her mind.

She reached into her pocket and rubbed the stub of cardboard there. Her eyes snapped open, and she knew what she had to do. She knew that Scott would never agree to it, and she knew that they had exhausted all of Maddie's options. She walked over to the cashier and asked for more change. With the quarters in her hand, she rushed back to the phone, worried that someone else would hop on it before she got back, and then she'd lose the nerve to do what needed to be done next.

But when she got there, the phone sat vacant, its polished chrome shining under the fluorescent lights of the hospital. She pulled the torn remains of the business card from her pocket and set them on the metallic shelf of the phone. Angela arranged the edges until they were just right, fitting together like the edges of a jigsaw puzzle. She lifted the receiver, took a deep breath, inserted her coins, and dialed the number on the card. Her heart beat in her chest. *What if he changed his number? What if he found someone else? What if this is all a prank?* The thoughts tumbled through her head, and her ears flushed warm with blood as her heart began beating faster.

It rang. It rang again. *It's too late. He's a young guy. Maybe he's out at the bar. Maybe he's working at the hospital.* On the fourth ring, as she was about to hang up, she heard a click and a rustling. "Hello?" she asked, hating the desperation in her voice.

"Hello?" a querulous voice responded.

"Mr. Brewster? It's me, Angela. We met a few weeks ago." *God, has it only been a few weeks?*

She could picture him straightening his glasses as his mind began to work. She could picture that round face, that pouty lower lip that always looked so pink and moist. "Oh, yes... Angela. I didn't think I would ever hear from you after what happened at your house."

She didn't want to think about it. She didn't want to think about the time they had wasted. *Maybe it's already too late.* "Yes, well. Things are different now."

Concern edged into Brewster's voice as he asked, "How different?"

"Maddie..." She paused, searching for the right words, because she didn't want to say them. She didn't want to taste them on her lips. "Well... she's in a coma right now." She heard Brewster suck air through his teeth. She continued, "And the doctors don't think she's going to wake up from it."

"I'm sorry to hear that, Angela." The condolences almost sounded genuine, as if there was a real person inside of Brewster. That felt reassuring to her.

"Is there anything that you can do?"

There was no pause, no hesitation, as Brewster said, "I can save her, Angela. I can save her life." It was good that he didn't hesitate. If he had hesitated even a moment, she would have lost her nerve. She would have hung up right then and there and pretended that she had never even made a phone call to the young scientist.

"How?" she asked because she had to, because she knew that Scott might still refuse Brewster's help.

"I can't tell you over the phone. It's all... very technical. It's best that I meet you in person, and it sounds like there isn't much time. Am I correct?"

Angela nodded, feeling stupid because she knew that Brewster couldn't see it. "Very," she said.

Brewster sounded electric over the phone. "Then we had better schedule the meeting now. Tell me, Angela, does your husband know you're calling me?"

"No, he can't know." And it suddenly dawned on her, that she was willing to go through with Brewster's treatment, with or without Scott.

"That's a bit of a problem. You see, for this treatment, I'm going to need the permission of both of you. It wouldn't be ethical if I did it any other way. It also might not work at all. You two are an important part of the cure."

She knew Scott... she knew he was broken. "He's never going to agree to meet with you. He's already so angry and bitter."

"All the more reason for you to convince him, Angela. All the more reason. Listen, when he agrees to meet with me, call me right back. I'll be readying my things. We can meet wherever you want to, but the sooner I get permission from both of you, the sooner we can get under way. Do you understand, Angela?"

"Yes," she said, not because she believed she could convince Scott, but because this was Maddie's only shot. "I'll call you right back." She hung up the phone, the wheels turning in her head. She stood there, her hand sitting on the receiver... thinking, feeling hopeless.

****

In the hospital room, Scott sat, wondering where his wife went. He held his daughter's hand, gripping it, hoping that at any moment, she would grip his hand back. He couldn't have her die like this, disappearing without a chance to say goodbye. She had to hear him at least one more time. She had to hear him say, "I love you." He had to be able to tell her that there was a heaven, and that there would be family members there waiting for her, and that one day, he, her mom, and Clayton would find her there, and they would all be together again. He believed this now more than he ever had in his life because if there wasn't a place where they could all be together… well, he didn't want to think about that.

Where is Angela? She should have been there. It wasn't right, her disappearing like that. Maddie could... she could go at any minute. A mom should be there. He clenched his jaw, and tried to remind himself that grief took all forms. Fear was one of them. Avoidance was one of them. But dammit, he expected better of her. She was the strong one. She was the one that held them together.

Just as he was about to get up and go find Angela, the door to the room opened. Angela came in. She looked skittish, nervous, like a dog with its tail tucked between its legs after it had pissed on the carpet. He had seldom seen her like that. She was always so cool and calm; even when he lost his own temper, she was always there to bring him back down.

"What's wrong?" he asked, noting the barely perceptible twitch of her body at his words.

"Nothing," she said. She pulled a chair next to him and sat. Then she leaned forward and placed her hand over his and Maddie's hands. They were all joined as one. It felt good. Her hands were soft, but he could feel a slight tremor. They sat that way for a while in silence. His mind wandered, thinking of heaven, hell... thinking of how he was going to break the news to Clayton. He tried to imagine the scene in his mind. Scott envisioned himself being strong and tear-free for Clayton. Then he imagined something that would be closer to reality, him sobbing like a baby and cradling Clayton in his arms. He squeezed his eyes shut and tried to shake his thoughts.

Scott tried to think of Maddie at her best, sliding into third-base in her final little league game. He had tried to make her an athlete, but it just wouldn't stick. She didn't have the competitive edge that he had. She was cool like her mother. But for that one moment, he had seen that look on her face, that look you see on the faces of athletes on the edge of greatness, pure determination and desire. From the third-base line, he'd had a perfect view of her face as she dove head-first into third base– something you weren't supposed to do in little league– as she hustled to beat the cut-off throw from the outfield.

It was a great memory. She had come up with a scraped-up chin, blood dripping from it, all smiles, dusting off her uniform. She had quit little league the next year, but he would always have that moment, with the sun shining down on a June day.

The memory burst like a bubble as Angie spoke. "I called that scientist," she blurted out, and instantly he understood why she had come in with her tail tucked between her legs.

"What? Why?" he blurted out.

"I know, I know," she said, cutting him off. "But don't you think we ought to look into it? Don't you think we ought to hear him out? If there's a chance, some small chance that he can save Maddie, don't you think we ought to do it?"

"The guy's obviously a quack, Ange. He's probably just looking to make a quick buck off us."

"Great, so we just sit here and let our daughter die."

"That's not fair. That's not what I'm saying at all."

"You're not saying it, but it's the same thing."

Scott looked his wife in the eye, and he could see that she wasn't going to let this go. She shouldn't. She was right. As much as he hated to admit it to himself, he wasn't ready to just give up. He had no hope that this scientist was going to be anything other than a snake oil salesman, but he saw that Angela was not going to drop the matter. He could tell by the set of her jaw that she was going to go through it with or without him, and God help him if he didn't go along. "It's not the same thing," he said, though he knew his argument was futile.

"All you have to do is listen," Angela said. "What does it hurt to listen?"

"It already hurts bad enough," he whispered. "The last thing we need is some quack giving us false hope. And that's all this guy is, Angie. He's just a quack, a snake oil salesman preying on people who've got no place left to turn."

"So? What if he is? All we have to do is listen. If he sounds like he's full of shit, we send him on his merry way and get back to life. We're back to our normal miserable selves, waiting for our daughter to wither away before our eyes. It's not like the situation could possibly get more miserable." She paused then, and her words rattled around in Scott's skull, battering against his heart, which was telling him that everything about the situation was totally wrong. "But what if he isn't a snake oil salesman? What if he can do what he says?"

Scott looked at his wife, and he could see the hope in her face. He resented it because he didn't feel a shred of hope within his entire body. "I'm scared," he finally admitted, hating for the hundredth time that she was the strong one, and he the weak.

Her face softened, and she stroked his hand softly. "Of what?"

"Getting my hopes up."

Her hand moved to his face, rasping across the stubble on his cheek. "There's nothing wrong with being scared, and there's nothing wrong with having hope, Scott. But you should have heard the way he said it. '*I can save her.*' There wasn't a doubt in his mind. At the very least, we can listen."

Scott squeezed his eyes shut, and somewhere, in his chest he felt a small coal of hope fanning to life. He opened his eyes and looked at Maddie's sunken face. But that wasn't the face he saw. He remembered the blood on her chin, the dirt on her uniform, and the determination on her face. "Give the man a call," he sighed.

Angela was up out of the chair quicker than a cobra strike. He grabbed her hand just before she was out of his reach. She turned to look at him. "But I can't promise I won't punch his lights out if he wastes our time."

She smiled at him. "No one is asking you to promise, babe."

He nodded at her, and she left to make her phone call.

Chapter 5: The Meeting

The hospital chapel was draped in silence, a sad somber place. Decorated in dark woods and dim lighting, it felt not like a holy place, but like a place outside the stream of time. The pews were made of dusky wood, shiny and lacquered smooth. Above them, behind the pulpit, loomed a gray, clay statue of Jesus, shirtless and crucified. Its eyes were smooth, pupil-less, and Scott thought that if the statue were to come to life, he would run in fear from it.

For the moment, they had the chapel to themselves. There was no priest in sight, which suited Scott just fine. Men of the cloth all gave him the creeps, except for Father Romero. A flash of guilt made him momentarily embarrassed. He shouldn't have talked to Father Romero the way he had. It wasn't right. All he had been trying to do was help. He vowed to apologize to him when he had the chance.

Angela sat pensively, chewing on a thumbnail. They had nothing left to say to each other. They had used up all of their words. Now all that was left to do was wait. He unclenched his hands after realizing he had been making fists so hard that his own fingernails had been digging into his palms. His mouth felt dry, and he looked at the statue of Jesus again. He said a little prayer to the alien-looking Jesus and his father above. It couldn't hurt, and while he was here, he might as well put in a word for everyone he knew.

He was in the middle of asking God to watch out for Clayton when the doors to the chapel burst open, and Liam Brewster came storming in. He was unkempt, as if he had just woken up and thrown on whatever was handy. His clothes were rumpled, and his curly hair seemed greasy and flat on one side. Under his arm, he carried a laptop and fumbled with several files. As Scott watched, Liam dropped the files to the ground, spilling photographs and papers everywhere.

"Jesus," Scott muttered under his breath, and then looked sheepishly at the statue of Jesus. *Sorry,* he thought.

"Sorry. Sorry," Liam muttered. His voice was wavery, nervous, like a middle school student before a classroom presentation. He stooped to pick up the papers and shoved them haphazardly into the file folders, not seeming to care what paper went where. He stood up and approached them, a faint sheen of sweat on his face. His chest swelled as he took a calming breath, adjusted his glasses, and then hesitatingly said, "I'm glad you called."

Scott had nothing to say. He was just there to listen. Angela, for her part, remained silent as well. Liam seemed to sense their mood, composed himself further and slid into the pew next to them. Scott was glad that Angela was between them. The small coal of hope in his chest seemed to be dimming by the second. This guy was just a boy. He had probably legally bought his first beer just a year or two ago. How could this boy succeed where the smartest, most experienced doctors and scientists had failed?

"Get on with it, Mr. Brewster. My little girl is dying in the other room, and if you waste even a moment of my time, there's going to be hell to pay." The words were harsher than he intended, but they didn't seem to bother Brewster. The scientist just looked at him as if he had said something very interesting.

"What an uncanny choice of words," the scientist said.

"What do you mean?" Angela asked. The back of Scott's neck tingled, and he suddenly didn't care to hear what Brewster had to say. But he promised his wife he would listen, so he held his tongue.

"I mean that Hell is precisely the reason that I'm here today."

Angela turned and glanced at Scott out of the corner of her eye, checking to make sure he wasn't going to explode. Scott swallowed his immediate desire to stand up and walk out, though he began to feel that his suspicions were correct. Liam was a snake oil salesman.

Liam adjusted his glasses again and said, "Listen, there's no easy way to soften up what I'm about to say." He paused and licked his pink lower lip. "Are you god-fearing people?"

"I don't think fearing is the right word," Angela began, but Brewster cut her off.

"But are you religious?" he asked.

"We go to church... although a lot of good that's done us," Scott added, wondering where this was all leading and giving a sheepish glance to the clay, alien Jesus.

"Do you believe in the devil?"

The question was just thrown out there like nothing, like asking "Do you like baseball?" For a second, neither Angela nor Scott spoke, and then the meaning of the question finally wormed its way into Scott's brain. *The devil? What does curing his daughter have to do with the devil?* He began to stand, pulling Angela by the arm. "He's a crackpot, Angie. Let's go."

"Wait!" Liam shouted, his voice edging into panic. Scott spared him a glance, just a single second's hesitation, but that's all that Liam needed to launch into a hurried speech. "I am not a crackpot. I am a scientist. Though I myself am not a religious man, I have seen the power of religion. I have seen its regenerative abilities."

Scott tried to pull Angie up, but she angrily shrugged out of his grip. "Are you talking about a miracle?" she asked.

"Quite the opposite. I'm talking about a curse." Liam could see the doubt grow on their faces. He held a finger in the air, imploring them to wait one moment before they left. "I have something to show you." He pulled his laptop out, and as he booted it up, he said, "The popular idiom is that seeing is believing. After you see this, you might not think I'm so crazy after all."

"What is it?" Angela asked.

Liam paused and licked his lower lip again. "The answer that you're looking for."

****

The video played, and Angie's hand went unbidden to her mouth. Dark, wobbly footage played on the laptop's screen. Someone was holding the camera, obviously not a professional. In the gloom, Angie could make out a bed. On the bed lay a girl, not much younger than Maddie. She growled like an animal, gnashing her teeth. She looked rabid. Her arms and legs were covered in wounds. Her eyes were as black as coal, showing no whites at all. Blood trickled from the corners of her mouth.

The muscles in her arms and legs constricted as she tried to break free from the ropes that bound her to the bed. More blood seeped from her wrists and ankles.

The camera circled around the bed, and Angela began to feel woozy from all of the motion. The girl's head followed the camera, those obsidian eyes dully reflecting the candlelight in the room.

The child on the bed began speaking in a voice that no child had ever possessed. The words were strange, guttural, unfamiliar, but Angela could feel the hate in those words. The girl fell silent, and the camera moved forward and back as it tried to focus on her face. She smiled, exposing blackened teeth.

"I can feel her soul burning," the girl said in a breathy voice. If illness could be said to have a sound, it would be the girl's voice. It sounded like dried leaves and maggots crawling through flesh.

"What is this? A movie?" Angela asked. She was confused. She didn't know why Liam would show her this. She had never liked horror movies. She had banned them in the house, though occasionally, she would catch Scott watching one when he thought she wasn't paying attention.

"Just watch," Liam said.

A figure stepped into frame. He was an old man, blocky, square, his hair a uniform shade of silver. The person holding the camera stepped back to get the priest and the girl in frame. The camera's autofocus started to give Angela a headache. "Is that what you want? Her soul?" the priest asked.

The girl squirmed on the bed, in a way that felt almost sexual. "I already have it," the girl said. She began to laugh, a guttural choking sound.

"Then why are you still here?" the priest asked, his powerful, commanding voice cutting through the girl's laughter. He spoke with authority, a heavy, soothing voice.

The girl smiled, exposing her black teeth, her hands opening and closing above her head. "Because I want more."

The priest ignored the baiting nature of the girl's answer. "You'll be going home soon. You know that, don't you? But you won't be taking Katie's soul with you."

Katie. That must be the girl's name. Souls and priests. Angela was becoming more and more confused by the moment.

"There's nothing you can do," Katie spat.

The priest smiled then. "Oh, I know there's nothing that I can do." He points a finger in the air. "That's why I'll be calling on the help of the Lord."

At the word "Lord," Katie hissed like an angry cat.

The priest seemed to swell with satisfaction. "The Lord is here in this room. You sicken him. Can you feel his presence?" The priest didn't wait for an answer. Instead, he waved a small, brass wand held in his right hand. Holy water splashed forth from its end. The girl thrashed on the bed. "Tell me your name, demon!"

"I'll never tell," Katie said, though the mocking tone was gone from her voice.

The priest splattered her with more holy water. Where the water landed, it seared her flesh. The flesh split open like a hot dog on a grill for too long. Katie's insides were pink. The camera picked up a faint hint of steam rising up from where the holy water made contact with her skin. Very faintly, underneath the roar of Katie's pain, Angela thought she could hear sizzling.

"Give me your accursed name now!" the priest shouted. The speakers of Liam's laptop crackle with the power of the priest's voice.

Katie stuck out her tongue, black as night. She lowered her teeth onto the tongue, gnashing back and forth.

Scott could feel his stomach turning. He didn't know how much more of the video he could stand. He said, "This is disgusting. What does this have to do with Maddie?"

"Just watch the whole thing," Liam implored as blood began to ooze from Katie's tongue. Then the severed appendage dropped from her mouth. It wriggled on the bed, black ooze leaking from the severed end.

Angela felt nauseous. Bile rose in the back of her throat, but she kept her eyes on the laptop, watching the horrors play out on the screen. *There must be a reason Liam is showing us this.* "I think I'm going to be sick." The words escaped her, unbidden, a mere statement of fact.

On the laptop, the cameraman spoke, panic edging his words. "Did you see that? We need a doctor!

The priest turned to the camera, his eyebrows raised. "No doctor can help this girl. Keep recording. You wanted to see the Lord at work? Well, now's your chance."

The cameraman turned the camera away from the priest and refocused on Katie. The black tongue still wriggled on the bed, smearing black goo all over the white sheets. *They'll never get those stains out,* Angela thought. She didn't know where the thought came from, but she clung to it. It was either that or close her eyes, which she desperately wanted to do.

"Tell me your name!" the priest commanded. He plucked the tongue from the bed sheets and climbed onto the bed. The bed began to quake, its legs thumping on the wooden floor. The priest crawled up the girl's body, fighting the bucking bed, and then he jammed the tongue into the girl's face. Katie's head thrashed and fought him, but the priest was eventually able to force the severed tongue into her mouth. "I will have your name, and I will have it now before the eyes of the Lord and Jesus himself!"

Katie bucked on the bed. The bed mimicked her motion and the priest was thrown heavily onto the floor. The windows in the room shattered, spraying everyone with glass. The cameraman flinched away, but then brought the camera back to bear on the priest. White curtains billowed inward as an unseen wind swept the room.

The priest pulled a crucifix from his vestments. He leaned over the bed and pressed it to Katie's forehead. A scream like nothing Angela had ever heard erupted from the laptop. The hair on her arms and neck stood on end. She could see skin blistering as the camera zoomed in on where the priest pressed the crucifix to Katie's forehead.

Katie thrashed and screamed, "She will freeze in Hell with the rest of us!"

The priest stepped back and pulled a book from somewhere out of the camera's view. He began chanting, words that Angela couldn't make out. She felt them though. She felt the power in the words. Katie's wounds began to glow with a faint golden light. She howled in pain, the speakers of Liam's laptop crackling, unable to translate the sound data from the video. Angela was thankful for that.

"You're hurting me, father," Katie said, her voice taking on a tone that was sweet, innocent, and filled with pleading.

But the priest showed no mercy. "God allows me to see through your trick, foul beast."

"Please. I'm better now. It's gone."

"Prove it!" the priest spat. "Praise Jesus. Praise the Lord up above who banished the night creatures to the frozen bowels of Hell."

Katie's head moved from side to side, as she tried to form the words. Unable to, she simply muttered, "Damn your god."

The priest emitted a shout, a booming, thunderous shout. He spread his arms wide; a golden light flickered at first, then filled the priest's body. He squeezed his eyes shut as the shout continued, and when his eyes opened again, they were filled with the golden light. He raised his left arm in the air, and the light flowed like water, drawn to his closed fist until it was all concentrated there, shining. He brought his hand down in an open slap onto Katie's chest. There was a thunderclap, and her body shuddered as if she had been hit with a defibrillator.

Angela heard Scott say, "Oh, my god." Angela shared Scott's sense of awe, but she was unable to say anything.

"Tell me your name!" the priest shouted. Where the priest had placed his hand, smoke rose from Katie's chest. "The Lord is in me, and, through me, into your black heart. I know this pains you, demon. Now tell me your name, and I'll stop."

"Nooo! Stop! It burns!" Katie yelled, her voice on the edge of panic. The bed continued to rattle against the floor of the room. A wind blew through the room, pushing the curtains fluttering into the air as bits of leaves and branches from outside found their way inside. Plaster fell from the ceiling, and the priest dodged a large chunk as it crashed to the ground. A chorus of evil voices filled the room, dark whispering sounds, that Angela swore were actually calling her own name. She looked at Scott to see if he heard the same thing, but he was too enthralled with the video.

The priest raised his other hand in the air, and it too filled with a golden light. "I said tell me your name!"

Katie shook her head as the smoke continued rising from her chest, but she wouldn't say it, whatever was inside her wouldn't say its name. Angela clutched at her own chest, terrified for everyone in the video. The priest brought his other hand down, thundering into Katie's chest. The lights in the room exploded, shards of glass flying about the room. The camera took a moment to adjust to the darkness of the room, but the autofocus kicked in, aided by a haze of blue gloom that seeped in through the broken windows of Katie's room.

Katie screamed in pain.

The priest showed no mercy. He simply continued holding his golden hands over Katie's chest and saying, "All you need to do to stop this is tell me your name. Tell me your name, and this will all be over." His words were seductive. He spoke in the kind voice of a grandfather.

Katie screamed louder, as if her body was being torn apart from the inside. She thrashed frantically on the bed, but her strength was not enough to shake the priest or the golden aura that surrounded him. Blood, black and thick, sprayed out of her mouth and dripped from her eyes. The fingers of her bound hands carved furrows into the wooden frame of the bed.

Katie, or the creature inside her, could stand it no longer. "Silkerlax!" the creature wailed.

"Say it again!" the priest demanded.

"Silkerlax! My name is Silkerlax!"

The priest began to chant in the strange language again. Once again, Angela had the eerie feeling that she should know these words, though the words carried with them a feeling of antiquity. The priest never pulled his hands from Katie's body, and the golden light that suffused his body never wavered. His voice rose, his words flying so fast that he seemed to be saying multiple words at once. His eyes drifted closed as if he had gone to sleep. The priest's lips moved on their own as the rest of the muscles on his face became still.

"Release me!" Silkerlax yelled from within the mortal form of Katie.

The priest continued to chant. Katie's skin began to blacken. "Holy shit," the cameraman muttered absentmindedly. Katie screamed again.

Then all was quiet, but for the heavy breathing of the cameraman.

The priest, so loud, so commanding just a few minutes ago, parted his lips ever so slightly, and in an almost imperceptible whisper, he uttered the syllables... "Silkerlax."

Katie screamed once more. Her body flew upward as the ropes binding her snapped like Red Vines. She hit the ceiling, and Angela wondered how high she would have gone if there were no roof to stop her. Her body convulsed on the popcorn ceiling, blood streaming from her mouth and eyes. She screamed and her body spun.

Barely audible, the priest said the creature's name once again. "Silkerlax."

Black blood rained down upon the bed where Katie formerly lay, patterning the sheets like some sort of grim Jackson Pollock painting. The room flickered with holy light, golden, emitting from the priest.

"Silkerlax!" the priest bellowed, his cheeks seeming to quake at the command in his voice.

Katie, still squirming on the ceiling, began to claw at herself and shred her clothing. She opened gaping wounds on her own body, and more blood began to fall, peppering the image on the screen of Liam's laptop.

"Get thee back to hell!" the priest shouted.

Katie squeezed her eyes shut and bashed her head against the ceiling. Red foam built on her lips as she began to tremble. Her eyes opened; they were filled with a glowing red light. Katie screamed, and a blood-red aura, streaked with black, escaped from her mouth. Then Katie was falling, her body limp.

She slammed onto the bed, spraying more black blood onto the lens of the camera. The bed itself is cracked in half with a loud croak.

The red aura, expelled from Katie's body, encircled the priest's body, then flew into the priest's mouth. He gasped and fell to the ground. The cameraman rushed over to help Katie.

"Katie? It's alright, Katie. It's all over." The cameraman's words were soothing, but Angela was revolted by the fact that he didn't put the camera down.

Katie was still, unresponsive to the cameraman's words. "It's going to be alright," he said. Katie's eyes fluttered for a second, and then her eyelids popped open, and Angela found herself finally able to take a breath. The girl tried to strangle out a word, but nothing would come. She breathed deeply, sobbed, and rolled over. She reached out with an unsteady hand and grasped a fistful of the priest's robes.

The cameraman continued with his repetitious assurances, but Angela couldn't help but wonder if he even believed them. "It's alright, Katie. It's over. The nightmare is over."

The cameraman finally stopped focusing on Katie and pointed the lens in the direction of the priest. He lay still on the wooden floor, Katie clutching at his robes and sobbing.

"Are you alright?" the cameraman asked the priest. The cameraman finally put the camera down on its side, and the picture went dark abruptly.

Liam closed his laptop. Angela sat back, knowing that the look on her face must match the look of confusion on Scott's. "What the hell was that?" she asked. Her mind was spinning. The images she saw, the words and sounds she heard, had shaken her more than she could have ever believed. She didn't understand why Liam would show them this... this thing.

Scott echoed her sentiments and said, "I still don't understand what this has to do with Maddie."

Liam said, "What you saw was real. The film shows the exorcism of a girl named Katie Custary."

Real? How could any of that be real? Angela wondered.

"Oh, come on. You don't expect us to believe that was real," Scott said.

It's not real. None of it. It's just a movie, a really well-done movie. "Why would you show us this?" Angela asked.

Liam scrubbed his hand across his face, suddenly looking very tired. He adjusted his glasses once more, and then, as if speaking to the simplest of children, he said, "I'm showing you this because this is the answer."

"The answer to what?" Scott asked.

Liam ignored Scott's question and pulled a sheaf of papers from the folders sitting next to him on the pew. "Here." He waved the papers in Angela's face, as if they contained all of the answers. Angela grabbed them, unsure of why she didn't just walk out of the chapel.

She flipped through the papers, one by one, with Scott looking on over her shoulder. The first paper was a patient record. The name at the top read "Katie Custary" just like Liam had said. There was nothing out of the ordinary in the record. She flipped the paper to the bottom of the stack and was confronted with a picture of Katie smiling in the sun, holding a mountain bike upright, an oversized helmet strapped to her head. "It's that girl Katie," Angela said. Flip. She looked at a picture of Katie in a graduation gown, from high school presumably. More and more pictures of a happy, healthy Katie followed.

"I don't get it," Scott said, bewildered.

"She was the girl you saw in the video. Before she had her unfortunate incident, she was suffering from cystic fibrosis. She was, in fact, scheduled for a lung transplant when she started exhibiting bizarre symptoms."

"Bizarre?" Angela asked.

"Oh, you know, just your average teenager speaking in dead languages, floating through hallways, the usual."

Angela looked at Liam from the corner of her eye as she continued to examine the papers. She was beginning to get an inkling of what was coming, and she wondered how long Scott would continue to listen.

"You still haven't explained what this has to do with Maddie. She has cancer, not cystic fibrosis," Scott said.

"Look at her," Liam said, picking out a photo of Katie at random. She was at a zoo, and the smile on her face reminded Angela of Maddie. He held the photo up and forced Scott to look at it. "There's no sign of anything wrong with her. Not a thing." Angela looked at the photo again. She looked perfect. She looked happy. The smile on her face was the type of smile one could only make when everything was perfect. "Cystic fibrosis is a genetic disorder. There's no way to treat it. But after her incident, there was no sign of it. She hasn't so much as had a cold according to her medical history."

Everything was clicking into place, but Angela wished it weren't. She knew what was coming, but she couldn't make herself even think the words. "What exactly are you saying?

"If you want to cure your daughter, we need to put a demon inside of her and wait for it to change her physiology with its regenerative properties." Liam said it all so simply, so matter of factly, as if he were simply talking about giving Maddie an injection.

Scott was incredulous. "You want to put a demon inside of our daughter?"

Liam waved off Scott's concern. "No. No. I want to cure your daughter. Yes, it's somewhat of an... unorthodox cure, but at this point, I don't see any other alternative."

Scott's reaction was not what Angela would have expected. He leaned back in the pew instead of leaping to his feet and pummeling Liam Brewster. The look on his face was one of thoughtfulness, not rage as she expected.

"This is crazy," he said, his voice sounding far away.

"Life is crazy. This world is crazy. The things we do for love are crazy. But we do them anyway," Liam said.

Hearing Liam speak of love came as a shock to Angela. She was about to say as much when Scott turned to her. "What do you think, Angela?"

Angela didn't know what she was thinking. If what Brewster said was true... but no, it must be true. She picked up a picture of Katie Custary, smiling and petting a horse. She wanted to see Maddie do that one day. She wanted to see Maddie standing on her own, with a full head of hair, petting a horse, and smiling like there was no tomorrow. Such a simple thing to want, and yet, it was so far out of her reach. "What choice do we have?" she asked. She was defeated. She would do anything. She looked up at the statue of Jesus looming over them for the first time. She'd been avoiding its glare for a while she realized. It judged her. She knew it did, but she just wanted to see her daughter smile.

Scott, ever the pragmatist asked, "How much is this going to cost us?" It didn't matter to Angela. They would pay whatever they must to save their daughter's life.

Liam smiled at them then, turning and throwing an arm over the back of the pew in the most relaxed mood she had ever seen him in. He adjusted his glasses once more and in a rather cocky voice said, "I think you'll like the price, Mr. Cutter. I'll do it for free."

Chapter 6: Preparations

The next day, they began preparations for Liam Brewster's cure. Scott was home when the delivery men brought an electric bed to the house. He listened half-heartedly as they explained all of the functions of the bed. He was too busy wondering if he had gone crazy. After that, the ventilator was delivered. They tried to explain that to him too, but Liam claimed he knew how it all worked, so Scott had more time to spend wondering if he had gone insane. When they left, he flipped on the power switch and watched the pump inside go up and down as a hiss of air escaped from the facemask. They had several spare facemasks and tubes. His next few days would be filled with constantly changing them out and sterilizing them so Maddie wouldn't get a lung infection. After that, an EKG showed up, a stand that could be used to give Maddie I.V. fluids.

Liam brought a host of other equipment he said would be needed for tests. Scott didn't ask where all of the equipment came from or who paid for it. He just wanted to get the show on the road. When they were done setting up Maddie's room, it looked more like a hospital room than a teenage girl's room. Standing in the room left him feeling unsettled.

Finally, on the next day, they brought Maddie home, along with a pair of nurses to help oversee the transition. He stood by helplessly, holding his wife's hand as the nurses transferred his daughter from a gurney to her new bed. They put the mask on her face, hooked up the EKG, and spiked a vein to get the I.V. going, and still none of it felt real.

After checking her readings on the EKG, Liam took several blood samples. He tested her blood-pressure. It was a little low, but according to Liam, that was to be expected for the condition she was in.

Now, Liam was in the kitchen, spinning vials of his daughter's blood in a centrifuge. Scott spent his time staring at the blue waves on the EKG's screen. Up and down, up and down. He liked seeing them. He liked seeing proof that his daughter was alive because that meant she was still in there somewhere. He took another swig of his beer, still wondering if he had made a mistake.

Angela entered the room, a bundle of knitting in her hand. They had traded off watching Maddie several times throughout the day. The truth was that Scott would have never left her side if he didn't have to, but Angela deserved some alone time with Maddie. Angela sat in the chair next to him and arranged her balls of yarn and her knitting needles. He didn't know how knitting worked, but the practice drove him nuts, all that clicking and unknotting. He bit his tongue and prevented himself from saying something to Angela about the knitting. That was her thing, the thing she did to calm herself. He drank beer; she knit things. Maybe if she had ever graduated to something more complex than stocking caps or scarves, he could stomach her hobby a little better. Nah. He just hated the whole idea of knitting. He finished off his can of beer and leaned forward to set it on the wooden floor.

"What are we doing?" he wondered, his voice barely audible over the constantly running machinery in Maddie's bedroom.

"What was that, Scott?" Angela asked, the clicking of the needles never stopping.

He stood and cracked his back. "Nothing." He headed down to the kitchen to grab another beer. In the hallway, he spied a little boy peeking around the corner and looking at him. "What are you doing?" he asked playfully. Clayton disappeared from the doorway and into his room.

His beer became an afterthought, and he followed Clayton into his room.

When he rounded the corner and looked in the doorway, Clayton was nowhere to be found. "Clayton?" he called. No answer. From the closet, he heard a faint scuffling sound. He crept up slowly, thinking that Clayton was just playing a small game of hide from Daddy. Scott winced as the wooden floorboard creaked underneath his foot, but Clayton didn't give himself away any further. Then he was standing outside the door to the closet. He reached out for the handle, and in one smooth motion, threw the door open. "Yaaahhhh!" he screamed.

Clayton stood there terrified, screaming at him. But instead of bursting into laughter like he had done so many times before, the boy burst into tears. His mouth hung wide as slobber fell from his mouth, and he squeezed his eyes shut and wailed. Scott dropped to his knees, ignoring the pops of middle age. "What's wrong buddy?"

But Clayton was unable to answer. He gently pulled the boy to him, though at first, his son offered a small bit of resistance. He picked the boy up and set him on the edge of his bed.

"Shhh. It's all right Clayton. I didn't mean to scare you." He ran a hand over his son’s curly black hair, noting that Clayton was in dire need of a haircut. "Hey, we're just having fun."

For the first time, Clayton was able to close his mouth. He took a couple of deep hiccupping breaths, and then wiped his runny nose with the back of his sleeve. Scott waited patiently, rubbing Clayton's back until he seemed to gain control of himself.

"You want something to drink?" Scott asked. "You want some water?"

Clayton nodded his head without looking up at Scott. Scott went down to the kitchen, noting Liam fidgeting with one of his pieces of machinery. He pulled a plastic glass down from the cupboard. Clayton wouldn't drink out of glass cups, as he claimed he could smell the glass, and he didn't like the way it smelled. He pulled a pitcher of water from the fridge, filled it, and walked back up the stairs to find Clayton sitting on the edge of his bed staring down at his feet.

He held the cup of water out to Clayton, and he snatched it away with two hands. He set it on his lap for a moment, and then, without looking at Scott, he tilted it up to his mouth and drank the way four-year-olds did, deeply and quickly, so that by the time he pulled the glass away from his lips, he was absolutely out of breath.

Scott sat on the bed next to him, running a hand over Clayton's skinny back. "Is that better?"

"Yeah," Clayton said meekly. He tilted the glass up to his mouth again and finished off the rest of the water.

"You think you can tell me why you got so scared just now?"

Clayton shook his head from side to side and then fell backwards on his bed, looking up at the ceiling.

"Oh, no. You don't get off that easy." Scott grabbed an arm and pulled Clayton upright. The boy didn't resist. "In this family, when something is bothering us, we talk about it, and you know what?"

"What?"

"When we talk about it, we feel better. You want to give it a shot?"

"No."

"Aw, come on. Just give it a try. If you don't like it, I'll never ask you why you're crying ever again."

"Promise?"

"Promise."

Clayton looked up at him with red, puffy eyes. "I was just seeing if you could still see me."

His son's answer hurt him, made him feel like a real piece of shit. "What do you mean still see you?"

"Well, it's just that you guys have been sitting with Maddie all the time; it's like you don't even see me."

"No, we see you buddy. Didn't I see you in the hall?"

Clayton sniffs inward. "Yeah," he trembled. "But you didn't see me earlier."

"What do you mean earlier?"

"Earlier?"

"Like today?" The boy nodded his head. "Where were you earlier?"

"In the dryer."

"In the dryer? How long were you in the dryer?"

"For hours."

This was definitely what a piece of shit felt like. "Hey, I'm sorry. I guess we've been pretty busy around here. Maybe we haven't been paying enough attention to you."

"When I was in the closet, it felt like I waited for so long, that you weren't going to come and find me."

"Then I scared you."

"But I wasn't sad. I was happy, but I don't know."

Scott put an arm around his son's shoulders and squeezed him tight. "It's ok, Clayton. Sometimes it may seem like we don't see you because there's a lot of stuff going on around here, but I want you to know you're just as important to me as Maddie, as your mom. Even when you're not around, I'm still thinking of you. Ok?"

"Ok." Scott gave Clayton another squeeze and then picked him up in the air, noting how much he'd grown over the last few months, and though he couldn't admit it to Clayton, there had been times where he *hadn't* seen the boy. But he would never tell Clayton that. He made a silent promise to himself to spend more time with Clayton. *God, what if I'm scarring him right now? What if he grows up to think that he is unloved, that his parents didn't care about him because he sat inside a dryer for two hours and no one ever came to check on him?* "Hey, how about some ice cream?" It was all he could think to do. *But wait? Isn't that just teaching him to cope with his emotions by eating food?* There were times when he hated parenting as much as he had ever hated anything in his life. *Well, I already let the ice cream cat out of the bag.* Clayton's emphatic nodding let him know that there would be no stuffing it back inside.

"Come on, big guy." He held his hand out to his son, and Clayton grabbed it. For a moment, Scott marveled at how small Clayton's hand was. Clayton gave his nose another wipe with the shirt sleeve of his free arm, and together, they went downstairs and shared a bowl of Rocky Road ice cream.

****

Liam spun the focus on the microscope. The girl's white blood cell count was almost non-existent. It was a miracle that she hadn't succumbed to an infection, or at this point, even a common cold.

He recorded his data on a sheet and tried to ignore the father and son eating their ice cream in the kitchen. He silently wished they would just go away. People were not his forte, and family interactions even less so. He still wasn't sure what the little boy's name was. He was... inconsequential. Even as he had the thought, he placed a mental Post-it on it and filed it under "things not to say out loud."

Maddie. That was the girl's name. This all would have been so much smoother if the Cutters had agreed to the cure weeks ago. Oh, well. There was still time. Tomorrow would be a big day. To think that he would actually be involved in a demonic possession. It somehow excited him. He didn't believe in heaven or hell or demons, but he knew what the mind was capable of. Even now, he would bet that his readings in the morning would show improvement, simply from the aura of faint hope that permeated the house.

He was a hundred-percent sure of his cure. Well... maybe ninety-nine percent. But the Cutters didn't need to know that. They didn't need to know much of anything. They were living on a hope and a prayer, as the old proverb went. Yes, tomorrow would be when the hard work began. He slid a tube of Maddie's blood in a rack and placed it in the fridge.

The father, Scott, frowned at him for that. But what else was he to do? Bring his own refrigerator? He had already brought enough stuff as it was. The kitchen counter was barely large enough for the centrifuge. Scott didn't argue though. He had to see that arguing would be pointless. Yes, they weren't stupid this family. He found them quite intelligent on their own, although when they got together, they interacted in ways that made his skin crawl. But he could tough it out. He could do whatever needed to be done to see that his cure worked.

****

Angela woke up feeling exhausted. Despite the fact that she knew she needed sleep, she hadn't been able to make herself leave Maddie's side until a sleepyheaded Scott had come and basically dragged her off to bed, whereupon he took up the watch. Despite her long hours of watching, Maddie had never even stirred, not so much as a twitch.

Angela's sleep had been fitful, filled with nightmares of growling creatures with hideous forms. In one dream, she had been walking through her house, a trick of the dream making every step seem like a step backwards. The house had been empty, filled with a blue light that left her feeling chilled to the bone. After what seemed like an eternity of walking and getting nowhere, she called out for help, but no one answered. She continued to walk, and in the distance, she heard Maddie calling for her. "Maddie!" she called back, fear taking hold of her chest. She tried to run, but her limbs were sluggish, and the house seemed to move around her. She could hear Maddie's voice calling her, but she was unable to leave the upstairs hallway of the house.

She called for Scott and Clayton to help her. Only the eerie silence of the dream answered, and still Maddie's voice called to her. With each plaintive wail, the voice seemed to get farther and farther away, until it was as faint as a breath. Then a creature appeared, materializing out of thin air. It was humanoid in shape but surrounded by a gaseous black cloud that it wore like armor. From within the cloud, Angela could only make out a few small details. She had the impression of dozens of spikes and two glowing blue eyes. The creature crept towards her, and she screamed for help. Liam appeared behind the creature, but he paid her no attention as he kept transferring one liquid back and forth between two glass flasks. The creature stalked closer. Her dream voice went hoarse, until eventually, she could make no sound at all. As the creature reached out for her, with a hand composed entirely of black spikes, her eyes snapped open and she bolted upright, back in reality. Her body was drenched in sweat.

In a panic, she looked at the clock to see that it was nine in the morning. She had slept for six hours. *Long enough,* she thought. *Especially if all my sleep is going to be filled with nightmares.* She rose and walked through the house still dressed in the clothes she had worn the previous day. She hadn't had the energy to change before she went to bed.

Angela could feel that everyone was awake. As a parent, it was something that you learned early, that feeling of others up and about in your house. In Maddie's room, she found Clayton leaning on Maddie's bed with one of his Dr. Seuss books opened. Scott watched as Clayton read the story for his sister, and like that, the fear of her dream was dispelled. She shared a smile with Scott, but Clayton didn't notice her arrival. Angela didn't interrupt him as he stumbled over the words. He was just learning, but he was already further along than Maddie had been at the same age. He was such a bright boy. When he finished *The Fox in Socks*, he closed his book solemnly, and then he said, "I hope you wake up soon. You're better at reading than I am."

"I thought that was great," she said, and Clayton spun around, a small scream on his lips.

"You scared me!" he admonished her.

She walked over to him and picked him up. She gave him a crushing hug and then apologized for scaring him.

"Your breath stinks," he said with the precociousness that only a four-year-old could seem to wield with impunity.

"I suppose it does. How about I take a shower and then make us all some breakfast?" she said. Clayton liked the sound of that, so she placed him on the ground and he ran from the room, pretending he was Superman. "Any requests for breakfast?" she asked Scott.

"I'm sure whatever you make will be fine."

"And I'm sure whatever you make for dinner will be fine as well," she said as she walked off, a panicked look on his face. The truth was, there wasn't much food at all in the house, not anything that Scott could turn into dinner in any case. With Maddie's sudden turn for the worse, she hadn't been able to make it to the grocery store in some time. When Scott went to look at the fridge, he would find nothing that he could make... which meant pizza, which was honestly what she wanted for dinner. Pizza was her comfort food. When Angela was a child, and her mother and father had still been together, her father would always bring home pizza on Friday, that way her mother didn't have to cook. Scott, though a lovely husband, could be kind of lazy, and so on nights when she wanted pizza, she would just tell him that he was in charge of dinner, and inevitably, he would crack under the pressure and order pizza for the family. As an added benefit, it gave Scott a friendly reminder that she wasn't the only one responsible for the household duties around here, something of which he constantly needed to be reminded.

After a breakfast of bacon, eggs, and toast, she checked in with Liam to see what he was up to. He was still plotting data and looking at blood samples for various things that she didn't quite understand. Though he sounded like a professor, he was not exactly the best of teachers, and much of what he said went in one ear and out the other. He did produce a plastic necklace that looked like one of those little buttons that old ladies wore around their necks. *Help, I've fallen and I can't get up* is what she thought as soon as he pulled it from a pocket.

"With this," he said, "you can tell when there is something wrong with Maddie. If something happens, this will buzz and emit a loud beep, that way, you and Scott don't have to sit watch over Maddie every minute of every day." He held it out to her. "I thought you should have it. You seem responsible for so much around here." She thanked him and slid the necklace on over her head. She had no intention of being away from Maddie, and she knew that Scott didn't either, but it was better to be safe than sorry she supposed. When she asked how much longer he was going to need her counter space, his only reply was, "For as long as Maddie is sick."

After that, she left him alone, which, by the unslumping of his shoulders, she thought he was grateful for. The rest of the day was uneventful, though after Scott told her of Clayton's crying incident the night before, she made some time to play with him. Despite how she had felt earlier about putting on the life alert necklace, as she was playing trucks with Clayton, she was reassured by its dangling presence between her breasts.

"Vroom!" Clayton squealed as he slammed a pickup truck into a dump truck. So much destructive energy. She wondered where it all came from. Eventually, she put Clayton down for a nap and relieved Scott from his watch. He stumbled from the room. *That one could also use a nap.* It was amazing to her how much energy it took simply to keep watch over someone. Before he left, she thought about giving Scott the necklace so that he would know immediately if something were wrong, but she held onto it, tucking it into her shirt so that it could touch her skin. It sat directly over her heart.

With that, she picked up her knitting, rustling the plastic bag to find the lead of her yarn. She didn't know what she was making; she didn't care. It would probably be another sock or hat, of which, everyone in the household had plenty. Maybe Liam could use a hat.

As the needles moved unconsciously in her hands, her body began to relax. Her knitting habit, as Scott called it, had been instilled in her in her teenage years. One summer day, she complained about not being able to go to the pool with her friends. "Pools cost money," her mother said. "And what do you get when you're done? Probably a sunburn and an infection from swimming in everyone's pee." So her mother had given her a hobby to fill her lazy summer days. At first, she resented it. She resented the fact that her mother didn't make enough money for her to do the things that all the other kids could do. When her parents had divorced, her life had changed, and everything had suddenly taken on a cost. As an added benefit, she had been able to make little things for herself that she wouldn't have otherwise had. This was especially beneficial in the cold winter months. Mittens, hats, and extra thick socks went a long way towards keeping warm. Knitting had become a part of her, and it was one of the few things that she could actually thank her mom for.

In addition to an appreciation of knitting, she also thanked her mom for showing her how to be a good parent. Her mother, strong and overbearing, had taught her a great deal about responsibility. She had taught her a great deal about doing what needed to be done. Yes, if there was one thing that she could say about her mother, it was that she had always done what needed to be done. Work two jobs to pay the mortgage? She did that. Beg, borrow, and steal to make sure that Angela had all the stuff she needed to keep up with the other girls in school? She did that as well. Her mother's ability to spot a deal had been legendary among the other mothers.

She also learned what not to do from her mother. She didn't hold her kids' mistakes against them. Angela's own mother had seemed to take pride in holding a grudge over her whenever she found her way into the occasional spot of trouble. She understood it now. Her mom was just trying to make her mistakes so painful that she would never make them again... but there was a better way than that. Angela took pride in the fact that she talked to her children. She didn't shame them for their mistakes. She talked their mistakes through with them. When Maddie was sent home from school for slugging a little boy that had pulled her hair, Angela had sat down and talked about it with her, let her know why the behavior was unacceptable. And then she forgave her, with a warning that it should never happen again... and it didn't.

She was thinking of other ways that her mother had helped her become a better parent when the doorbell rang. A moment later, Scott yelled up at her and Clayton, "Pizza's here!" She smiled. He was like clockwork that one. She was shocked at how fast the time had flown by, but the gurgling in her stomach let her know that, yes, it had been quite a while since she had eaten. She might have even dozed off a bit, judging by the progress she had made on Liam's hat. Yes, she was sure that was what she was making now.

Angela placed her knitting needles and the nascent hat on her chair for later. She walked over to Maddie and gave her a kiss on her cold, dry forehead and headed downstairs. The pizza boxes took up the rest of the counter space in the kitchen, along with Liam's equipment. The smell of the pizza made her mouth water, and she began producing plates and forks from the cupboards and drawers.

Clayton was already in the kitchen bouncing up and down like a madman and chanting the word "pizza" over and over again. "Get him a damn slice already," Scott said. She put a piece of pizza on the plate, along with a fork, though he was just as likely to sprout horns from his head as to use the fork. She handed the pizza to Clayton, and he rushed over to his spot at the table, flying into his chair so that the chair's legs cawed against the linoleum.

She put a slice on her own plate, and even though she was starving, she found that she didn't much feel like eating. Scott joined her, and they ate in silence, with the exception of Clayton who bobbed his head from side to side and hummed a nonsensical tune. She reached over and rubbed his hair, noting that he would need a haircut soon, and he smiled at her with a mouthful of chewed Hawaiian pizza.

"You gonna eat?" Scott asked Liam. "There's plenty to go around."

Liam looked at them in surprise, as if they had just appeared out of thin air. He turned back to his clipboard, jotted one last note, and stood up and stretched his back with a sigh. "Well, I am quite famished."

Scott gave her a look that said, "Can you believe this guy?"

Liam grabbed the last plate off the counter and threw a slice of pizza on it. He sat at the table, in the spot that was usually reserved for Maddie. Angela felt surprised at how much the scientist sitting in Maddie's spot bothered her, but she said nothing.

"I think we're ready," Liam said. "Now all we have to do is wait."

Around a mouthful of pizza, Scott said, "Wait? For what?"

Angela didn't like the sound of waiting. Maddie could die at any minute, any second. Panic edged into her voice, "We don't have time to wait."

Liam nodded. "We won't have to wait long. I have some help coming. I can't exactly do all of this on my own. But don't worry, I've got it covered."

His words rang hollow in Angela's ears. *Don't worry.* The past six months had been nothing but worry. "Help," he had said. "Help? What type of help?" she asked.

Before Liam could answer, the doorbell rang.

"Oh, that will be him," Liam said.

Scott gave Liam a dirty look and then wiped his face with a napkin. He rose from his seat and Liam and Angela followed him to the door. Clayton, unaware that anything was going on, stayed at his spot, humming his strange song and shoving more pizza into his face.

In the foyer, Scott reached out and opened the door. Angela held her breath, wondering who this new stranger could be. She let the breath out when she saw a familiar face standing at the door. Father Romero, with his angular face and lanky body, stood there smiling, all dressed in black with a black-brimmed hat on his head.

"Father Romero?" Scott asked confused. "What are you doing here?"

It wasn't the greeting that Father Romero was likely expecting, but he took it with grace and said, "I noticed you weren't at church the last few weeks. I just wanted to stop by and make sure that everything was alright."

"Oh... no, we're fine," Scott managed to say awkwardly, and Angela wondered just what Father Romero would make of Liam's cure. For a second, she felt the way she did when her mother had caught her filching cookies in the middle of the night.

For a moment, they lapsed into silence, and Father Romero waited on the doorstep, unperturbed by their awkwardness. Scott, realizing that Father Romero wasn't just going to disappear, stepped to the side and waved Father Romero into the house. "Come on in, Father."

Father Romero stepped into the house, doffing his broad-brimmed hat, exposing his silver hair. Angela took his hat and his coat from him and hung them on the coat rack next to the door.

"Thank you," he said.

He looked around, and it struck her that this was the first time that she had ever seen Father Romero outside of the church grounds. She had seen him at Easter Egg hunts, church services, and picnics, but all of those events took place on the church grounds. To see him here standing in her house felt like seeing one of your teachers at the grocery store... it just didn't seem right.

"You have a lovely home," he said in a voice both gracious and deep.

"Uh. Thank you. Come on in. We're all back here. You hungry?" Scott asked.

"Oh, no thank you."

"You sure?" Scott asked. "We have pizza."

They all walked back into the kitchen, taking their seats. Angela plopped Clayton on her lap to free up a chair for Father Romero.

"I really shouldn't. I get terrible heartburn these days, but uhh..." Father Romero looked longingly at the pizza and pointed to the slice on Angela's plate. "Is that extra cheese?" Angela could see his will breaking before her eyes.

"If there's one thing we've learned these last few months," Angela began, "it's that life's too short to not enjoy the little things... like extra cheese. Please. Help yourself."

Angela pulled another plate from the cupboard and handed it to Father Romero. With twiddling fingers, he poised his hand over the pizza, as if warring with himself. "I guess one piece wouldn't hurt." He placed a slice on his plate and then sat in the chair recently vacated by Clayton, who dumped his plate into the sink with a clatter.

"Are we going to have to listen to you preach?" Clayton asked.

"Clayton!" Angela admonished, but Father Romero just laughed.

Graciously, he said, "No, not today, young Clayton. Today, I'm just here to enjoy your company."

"Sorry about that, Father. Clayton, why don't you go get cleaned up for bed?"

"Ok!" Clayton yelled for no reason at all other than youthful exuberance. He spun on the kitchen's floor and took off running, his heels pounding through the house. Angela watched him go with a warm feeling in her heart.

"Don't forget to brush your teeth!" she yelled after him. There was no response as he pounded up the stairs to the second floor of the house.

Father Romero extended his hand to Liam, who was daintily eating the crust of a piece of pizza. He had been largely silent since Father Romero had appeared. "I don't believe we've had the pleasure," Father Romero said.

Liam shook Father Romero's hand. "No, we haven't. My name is Liam." Liam's response was clipped, formulaic, as if he were reading from a script.

But Father Romero was unflappable. "And how do you fit into this wonderful family, Liam?"

"Who me?" Liam asked, though it was obvious that Father Romero was speaking about him. Liam looked down at the remains of the pizza on his plate. "I'm a doctor."

"A doctor? For Maddie?"

Liam adjusted his glasses, and Angela could tell that he was nervous. "Yes," was his response.

"And how is Maddie?" Father Romero asked, pointedly making eye contact with Scott and Angela. Again, she had that feeling of being caught doing something wrong by a parent. No one spoke for a moment, and then Angela said, "Things have taken a turn for the worse, Father. She doesn't have long."

Her words hit Father Romero hard, and he sat back in his chair, his hands falling limply between his legs. He was thunderstruck for a moment, and then he looked at their faces in turn before he said, "I must say, you all seem to be taking it fairly well."

"The doctor seems to think he might have a cure," Scott said. Angela silently thanked her husband for saying the words. She didn't think that she could have been the one to tell Father Romero what they were up to. She really just wanted to run upstairs and hide. Part of her wished that Father Romero had never even showed up at their house.

"A cure for cancer?" Father Romero asked incredulously.

"A cure for everything," Liam said, all awkwardness gone from his voice. In every other instance, he was awkward, gawky even, but whenever conversation turned to his cure, he was as confident and well-spoken as a politician. She only hoped that he didn't fail to deliver on his promises in the same manner as a politician.

With suspicion in his voice, Father Romero asked, "And just what is this cure?"

"Oh, I'd doubt you'd understand it. The explanation can be very technical. It involves a sort of boosting of the immune system through metaphysical gestation, which will, in turn, burn out the cancer cells in Maddie's body." The explanation, which was really no explanation that anyone would understand, rolled from Liam's mouth.

"Metaphysical gestation?" Father Romero asked, obviously confused.

"Show him the video," Scott prompted.

"Are you sure?" Liam asked with some degree of doubt in his voice.

"Do it," Angela said. She couldn't stand it any longer. She would not hide what they were doing. She would not have Maddie's cure be a cloud that hung over the family.

Liam sighed and readjusted the glasses on his face. It was clear that Liam wanted nothing to do with Father Romero, but the choice wasn't his. In truth, Angela would be glad to have Father Romero's input on the matter. Liam stood up from his seat and headed off to the living room. She could hear him muttering under his breath as he searched through his equipment for his laptop.

Scott and Angela sat at the kitchen table in silence. Father Romero glanced at each of them in turn, unasked questions on his lips. Angela looked down at the untouched slice of pizza on her plate to avoid his glance. When Liam returned with his laptop, Angela was glad as it broke their awkward silence.

Liam set the laptop in front of Father Romero with no ceremony. He clicked a button, and the video began to play. Angela watched Father Romero as he beheld the horror of the video. His face, stony and angular, showed no emotion. He watched the entire thing without saying a word. When the video ended, they all sat around the table expectantly. Father Romero stood and walked into the living room, his mouth open a tiny bit, his hand pressed to his chest.

Angela followed him, worried that he was having a stroke. He was not a young man anymore. Father Romero plopped onto the couch, knuckling his chest with his left hand. "Are you alright, Father?"

Father Romero glanced quickly at her and then hastily averted his eyes. He spoke to a spot on the coffee table in front of him. "Oh, it's nothing. I think that the pizza has given me indigestion. That or God is punishing me for letting you two go astray."

Scott appeared, placing a comforting hand on Angela's shoulder. "It really is the only way, Father," Scott said.

"May I see her?" Father Romero asked querulously.

Scott and Angela shared a look. Scott shrugged at her. Angela looked over her shoulder to see Liam leaning against the wall between the kitchen and the living room. His expression was blank, as if he were merely watching rats in a maze.

"Sure," she said.

****

Father Romero stood at the doorway to Maddie's room, a pensive look upon his face. He could see her lying there, an oxygen mask on her face, an I.V. plugged into her arm. She looked worse than when he had seen her last. He cursed himself for not coming sooner. *What have the Cutters gotten themselves into?*

The elderly priest stepped into the room and walked over to Maddie. He knelt next to her bed and took her hand in his. A prayer came unbidden to his lips, as one usually did when he needed it. He was not one for forms, and he knew that God was more about the sentiment, the earnestness of a prayer. Besides, if a person had to hear the same thing every day from hundreds of millions of people, it would literally drive them nuts. He knew from experience. All those times listening to confessions... if he never had to hear the words, "Bless me father, for I have sinned" again, he would count himself a lucky man.

He prayed for Maddie. He prayed for Scott and Angela. He prayed for Clayton. Though he didn't know him and didn't feel like he was going to like him, he prayed for the boy, Liam. When he was done, he asked God for forgiveness for his laxity in watching over the Cutters. He made the sign of the cross, and then he stood up. Feeling a little self-conscious, a little embarrassed for himself, he regarded Scott and Angela. Then he said what he would have said if they had come to him about the cure in the first place, "Scott, Angela... I forbid you to go through with this." He could see them about to protest, but he bulldozed right over them, not giving them a chance to argue. "I don't normally interject my beliefs into the lives of my congregation, but this is a matter of the soul."

Liam spoke then. "I showed you the video. You've seen the results for yourself."

The boy just didn't understand. He couldn't. He was a lost lad, clad in his belief in science. "What good is saving her body if you damn her soul to hell?" Father Romero asked.

"Can we do this somewhere else?" Angela asked, her eyes on Maddie.

Father Romero understood not wanting to speak about this in front of Maddie, even if she was in a coma, but it had to be said. "We cannot do this anywhere. This charlatan," he said pointing a finger at Liam, "is playing with forces that he cannot and does not understand."

Liam responded to Father Romero's tirade with an unimpassioned voice, "What is there to understand? Their little girl is dying, and I have a way to save her."

"You only seek to save the body," Father Romero implored, "but we are more than that." His mind grappled for some way to break through to the young man.

Liam turned to the Cutters and said, "Scott, Angela, I don't have time for this. I still have some baseline data to compile, and there's still plenty to do." Angela and Scott seemed torn between Father Romero and Liam.

The father, yes, the father would listen to reason. "Scott, I forbid you to do this."

"It's not your choice, Father," Scott said, his voice sounding far away.

Seeing no aid from Scott, Father Romero turned then to Angela. "Angela, surely you can see how wrong this is."

Angela didn't look at him directly. She continued to stare at Maddie, as if the girl were going to wake up at any moment. "I just want my little girl back."

Father Romeo's body ached with frustration, he grimaced at Scott and Angela. He knew that no matter what he said they were going to go through with Liam's cure. He sighed and wiped agitatedly at his brow, where a surprising amount of sweat had collected. "Very well. If you plan on going through with this, then I'll stay."

Angela said, "Father, we can't ask you to do that."

Then Scott chimed in. "Maybe it would be better if you leave, Father. I know how uncomfortable you must be with all of this, and I can't say that I blame you."

Father Romero nearly laughed. "You think if this 'scientist' opens the doorway to Hell that he's going to be able to seal it back up again? Ha! It's more likely that he will open the door, and what's inside will swallow you all whole. I can't allow that to happen." He straightened his garments and gave them a look that said there would be no arguing. "I stay."

Liam immediately protested and said, "Scott, I'm not sure this is such a good idea. He's only going to get in the way."

Father Romero had had enough of Liam. "The only one in your way is yourself. Are you so blind that you can't see what this cure of yours really is?"

"Stop," Angela said softly.

Liam did not hear. "This is the only chance they have. If God won't help them, then maybe the devil can."

"Stop it!" Angela yelled.

But Father Romero didn't listen, and for that matter, neither did Liam. They began yelling at each other. Father Romero was intent on putting Liam in his place, but Liam had no intention of backing down. They shouted so loud, that no one heard the doorbell at first. But upon the second ring, they all stopped.

"Who could that be?" Angela asked.

"My help," Liam said.

Father Romero's stomach dropped. He offered up a silent prayer as Scott, Angela, and Liam ran downstairs to see who was at the door.

****

Scott rushed downstairs, still shocked at the confrontation between Liam and Father Romero. They had been behaving like children, and there was nothing that Scott could do to stop them. He had stood there helplessly, wishing that they would stop, but if it weren't for the doorbell, he felt like it might have come to blows. He wouldn't have that, not around Maddie. If the two started arguing again, he would ask Father Romero to leave.

He pulled the front door open to reveal a man standing on his doorway. He had a head of brownish-gray hair, loose and wavy. He dressed all in black, the front of his dress shirt split in half by a skinny red tie. His sleeves were rolled up to reveal arms covered in tattoos, sinister faces with mouths filled with sharp teeth.

"Hello," the man said good naturedly, "my name is Matt." The man extended his hand then, and Scott shook it with only a slight sensation of unease. Matt peered around Scott and made eye contact with Liam.

"It's ok; he's with me," Liam said. Scott, still feeling unsure about the man, stepped to the side and let Matt enter the house. He noticed a black medicine bag in the man's hands. Scott turned to Liam and asked, "Who is this?"

Matt just smiled graciously.

Liam, adjusted his glasses, and right away Scott knew he was not going to like the answer. "This is the Satanist that's going to help us cure Maddie."

Angela's hand went to her chest. "Why would we want a Satanist here?"

"We need him for the possession," Liam said, as if it should have been common knowledge.

"Why can't you do it?" Angela asked.

"I know all of the particulars. That's true. I technically know how to perform the ritual, but there's just one little problem," Liam said.

"What's that?" Scott asked.

"Faith," Liam said. "I don't have any, so we need Matt."

Scott turned back to look at Matt. *A Satanist. In his house... around his kids.* Scott didn't like the idea, not at all.

Matt seemed to sense his concern as he said, "You have nothing to worry about. I'm not a bad guy. Really. The ninth rule of Satanism states that I shall do no harm to children. Do you want to know what the third rule is?"

"What?" Angela asked.

"When in another's home, show them respect or do not go there." Matt stated the rule with a slight bow in Angela's direction.

Scott was surprised by the rules. They didn't seem anything at all like what he would expect from a Satanist. "Sounds reasonable," he said.

Everything and everybody was calming down when Father Romero stormed into the room. "Get out!" he yelled, pointing emphatically at the door.

"Oh, look, a sheepdog," Matt said drolly.

"Father," Scott implored, "you said you were here to help. This is not helping." He felt bad calling Father Romero out, but they couldn't afford to be at each other's throats any longer, not with Maddie in her current state.

Angela backed him up and said, "Father, this is our house. If we want him here, then he's welcome here."

Father Romero wouldn't back down. "Angela, you don't know what you're doing. I understand that you want your daughter back, but this is not the way."

Scott almost felt sorry for Father Romero. He clearly thought he could change their minds, but there was zero chance of that now. "We've tried all of the other ways. This is all that's left."

"I can't talk you out of this, can I?" Father Romero asked.

Scott just shook his head, as Angela said, "No."

Father Romero nodded then, defeat on his face. He turned without uttering a word, stalked into the living room, plopped down on his knees, and began praying. Liam just looked at Father Romero and shook his head the way a father might at a particularly precocious child.

Then he shrugged his shoulders, and Liam said, "Yeah. Well. Shall we get to work?" Scott and Angela nodded, and Liam turned to Matt. "What do you need from us, Matt?"

"Just some time and a few extra hands," Matt said. "Oh, and as many candles as you can find."

****

Scott was busy lighting candles when Angela came back from putting Clayton to bed. Matt, the Satanist, had said that it would be dangerous to have two children in the house during the ritual, but if he stayed in his bedroom, he should be alright. Maddie's room was lit by the golden light of dozens of candles, and the room had become uncomfortably warm. Scott wiped sweat from his brow as he and Angela grabbed the last bunch of candles.

Matt entered the room with a jar of dark liquid and a paintbrush. "You're going to have to re-paint the room after this," he said.

"Is that blood?" Scott asked, eyeing the jar distastefully.

Matt looked at the jar, realizing perhaps for the first time, that it was not something that people just had on hand. "Yes. I got it from a friend of mine."

Dark thoughts ran through Scott's brain, pictures of Matt draining the blood from a helpless victim bound to a stone slab. Matt, as if he could read Scott's mind, said, "He's a butcher. It's pig's blood."

"Oh," Scott said, feeling sheepish.

Matt gave him a wink and a smile that said it was alright. Scott thought the Satanist was surprisingly nice for, you know, worshipping Satan and all.

Matt climbed a ladder and began scrawling symbols on the walls. Scott did not recognize any of the symbols. He and Angela grabbed a handful of candles and moved around the room setting them up. They had placed candles on the floor, on Maddie's dresser, on her nightstand. Together, the candles formed a circle of light, and by the time he had finished placing and lighting the last one, the room had become unbearably hot. Matt climbed down from the ladder, and Scott looked at the walls of the room. The symbols gave him shivers, despite the heat.

"Is all of this really necessary?" Scott asked.

Matt, surveying his work, said, "I can't say for sure. I mean... this is the way the rituals are laid out. Blood for the symbols, fire to represent the comfort of hell." He trailed off and looked at Scott before he spoke again. "But to be honest, I've only ever read about this particular ceremony. I've never actually been a part of one."

"You've never done this before?" Angela asked, somewhat panicked.

Matt looked at her with a mocking grin on his face. "Just because one learns of a way to kill a person with their bare hands, that doesn't mean they run right out and test it out on the first person they find. This ritual is not something that I would ever use. It is designed to harm people. But in this case, it will be used to save someone."

Scott nodded his head. It was reassuring to know that Matt wasn't evil. He didn't agree with the Satanist's beliefs, but he didn't seem all that different from himself.

"So now what?" Angela asked.

"Now I'm going to step out front, have a smoke, and then we'll begin."

****

Matt Richards stood on the porch, a cigarette burning in his hand. The sky darkened ever so slowly. It was almost the right time. He wished he could do the ritual in the daylight, but the strength of demons ebbed in the sunlight. Part of him was terrified of what he was about to do, but the other part of him was thrilled to be able to actually do some good with his knowledge. That's all he had considered it before, knowledge. He studied Satanism, the occult, and its rituals the way some academics studied dead languages. He was just trying to keep them alive. Just because some of the darker elements of the religion were unfavorable at the moment, that didn't mean they should disappear altogether. He had always endeavored to preserve

Satanism, like past scholars had preserved Latin or Sumerian.

Matt didn't believe in Satan per se, but that wasn't a necessity of the religion. His was a religion of questioning, of realism, of acknowledging the darkness that resided in all people, even those of the Christian faith. While there were many within that religion who were hopelessly lost, there were also many who were genuine good people, like the people inside. He could feel their love in the air. You could tell when you walked into a house whether it was a place of love, and the Cutters had it.

He had hope that Liam's plan would work. He took a deep drag off the cigarette and remembered his first meeting with the young man in his church, a dimly lit repository of books and ancient rituals. His flock was a quirky bunch, but he loved them just the same. As his black mass ended, Liam had approached him, looking rather sheepish and somewhat skittish. He understood the look. Many people had come to his church curious and yet fearful at the same time, fearful that he would attack them or demand a sacrifice or some other such nonsense. Oh, for sure, sacrifices were part of many of the ancient rituals, but blood magic was a dark powerful thing, and not to be undertaken lightly.

Matt had to hand it to the kid though. His plan just might work. All he had to do was keep the priest from meddling. He didn't like that the priest was here, but the Cutters seemed to have him on a short leash. Maybe he could help when the time came to banish the demon.

Jesus, I'm really doing this. The words tumbled round in his head until they stopped making sense.

He took the last drag from his cigarette and blew the smoke into the air, wondering what would happen to his little church if he were actually successful. He turned and headed back inside, ready to do the deed.

****

Matt stood in the room, double-checking the glyphs, the candles, the layout of the room. He was aware of the eyes upon him.

"It's time. I need you all to leave," Matt said.

Scott laughed a little bit, thinking the man was joking. But Matt just stared at him. "You're serious?" Scott asked.

"Deadly," Matt replied.

Angela spoke before he had the chance to, but she said exactly what Scott was thinking. "If you think we're leaving a Satanist alone in this room with our daughter, then you're out of your mind."

Matt seemed about to say something when Liam strolled into the room with a camera in his hands. "Don't worry," he called. "I knew you guys might have a problem with the set-up, so I borrowed this camera from the A.V. department at the university."

Liam dropped the legs on the tripod attached to the camera. He set it at the rear of Maddie's bedroom, against the wall. The positioning of the camera would provide the best view possible. "Once we set this up, we can see everything that's going on in the room."

"Can't we stay?" Angela asked.

Matt reached out and placed a hand on Angela's shoulder and looked her in the eye. "Your connection with God is enough to keep the demon at bay. It might not work if you're here." Matt removed his hand from Angela's shoulder and rubbed his fingers together as if he had just touched something distasteful.

Though Scott didn't like it, he was at the mercy of Liam and Matt. They knew how this all worked. He grabbed Angela by the shoulders and ushered her out of Maddie's room. "I don't want to leave. That's my little girl in there," Angela said, resisting his prodding. But she went anyway. Behind him, Liam closed the door.

Inside the room, Matt muttered to himself. "It's about damn time."

Chapter 7: The Ritual

Angela, Scott, and Liam rushed downstairs, passing Father Romero without a word. The elderly priest still knelt on the carpet in the living room, his hands clasped together, muttering unintelligible prayers. In the kitchen, Liam had set up a monitor on the kitchen table. On the screen, they witnessed Matt standing with his back to the camera, the room lit by the golden glow of dozens of candles. Maddie lay on her medical bed, unconscious to the world.

Matt began chanting. His words were guttural, almost animal-like, in a language that Angela didn't understand. But she felt the words, like a layer of filth and grime on her skin. The hair on the back of her neck stood up, and she felt the power in the words, a dark power, a power that, under normal circumstances, she wouldn't want in her presence.

"We must be out of our minds," Scott muttered. He paced back and forth, his arms crossed against his chest, casting glances at the monitor with each circuit he did in the kitchen. Liam leaned against the kitchen counter, watching the monitor with wide eyes.

"How do you even know this guy?" Scott asked.

"He has a church in town," Liam said.

Angela could hear the hard edge in Scott's voice as he said, "Do you believe it, Ange? A church."

She ignored his angst. It was the best thing to do. His edginess was a fire and acknowledging it in any way would only feed the flames. "Look!" Angela shouted. The image on the screen flickered, a brief haziness and swirl of static. "Did you see that?"

Scott stopped pacing for a second, then shook his head. "It's probably just faulty equipment." But he stopped pacing, his eyes scrutinizing the images on the screen. Liam licked his lips, leaning closer to the monitor.

On the screen, Matt continued chanting, his voice rising higher and higher. The image flickered once more, popping with static and fading for a moment. Angela, eyes glued to the screen, can't resist pointing at the monitor. "There. I saw something." Maybe it was just her imagination, but for a moment, just a split second, she thought she saw a shape hovering above Maddie's bed.

No one answered her. They had all fallen quiet, their eyes glued to the screen. The chanting continued, evil words, dark words. Scott, chewing on a thumbnail, concern etched on his face, blurted out, "No... no, this isn't right."

The image on the screen flickered once more, as did the lights in the kitchen. Angela was sure about it now. There was a shape, more distinct this time, a dark shape, composed of spines. It looked like the one from Angela's dream, only without the glowing red eyes. It hovered in the air above her child, and she put her hand to her mouth, unable to speak. Her scream stayed in her chest, but it was there.

Liam's mouth had dropped open. "It's working," he said in awe, as if he had never actually believed that any of this would actually be possible.

Scott couldn't handle it anymore. "This has to stop." He ran from the room, his eyes wide with terror.

"Wait! This is her only chance!" Liam yelled, but Scott didn't listen as he pounded up the stairs.

Angela could only sit and watch with horror as Matt continued chanting, and the flames from the candles flickered in Maddie's room.

****

Scott sprinted down the hallway to Maddie's room. *It's not too late. I can stop this.* He heard the muffled chanting coming from Maddie's room. He felt a wind rushing through the house. It carried the faint scent of spoiled meat. The wind alone was enough to confirm in his mind that he needed to stop the ritual. He placed his hand on the door handle and pressed it down, but it didn't turn. He looked at it for a moment in disbelief, attributing its unwillingness to budge to something otherworldly, and then he realized that Matt must have locked the door.

"Open this door!" he bellowed. He pounded on the door to punctuate his command, but Matt continued chanting.

****

Liam and Angela did not talk as they watched the monitor. There was nothing to say. They did not have the words to describe what was happening. From upstairs, Angela could hear Scott banging on the door, cursing and screaming, but they did not move to help him. The monitor held them in place, mesmerized.

Every so often, the image flickered. The shape, which had first appeared as something like a gaseous shadow, had solidified into a nightmare. It hovered for a moment over Maddie's body, and then it descended, enveloping her child in its blackness.

Angela's hand went to her mouth, and she watched the monitor through unspilled tears. Liam said nothing. He stared at the screen with his mouth open, and for the first time since she had met the young man, his lower lip actually seemed dry.

A wind rushed through the house, sending a pile of bills that Angela kept meaning to file flying through the air. The lights flickered, and a rancid smell assaulted her nose. From the living room, Father Romero began to pray even louder, his words rising to a hoarse bellow. Upstairs, Scott continued pounding on Maddie's locked door.

****

Scott stood in the hallway covered in sweat. His knuckles were bloodied from trying to punch through the door in his frustration. He didn't understand; it should have broken by this point. It was a cheap door. He should have been able to punch right through it, but when he pounded on it, it was if the door were fashioned out of steel. His bloody knuckles could attest to that. His legs ached from trying to kick the door open, but it hadn't even rattled with the blows from his boot.

Scott was still trying to puzzle out what was going on when he felt a presence behind him, a small disturbance in the air that would indicate that someone was there. As he turned to see who it was, the lights in the house flickered. A cold, noxious wind flooded down the hallway, and blasted him into the door. The back of his head hit the cheap wood and his world was turned off like a light switch.

****

In the kitchen, Angela could hear Matt's voice as if he were standing right next to her. His voice had risen to a fevered pitch, and it echoed with power throughout the house, as if amplified by speakers. She put her hands to her ears as the cold wind blew through the house, and Father Romero's voice rose in prayer to try and match the power of Matt.

On the screen, the image darkened steadily as the candles blew out one by one. She could barely make out the shadow of Matt's body and the shape of Maddie on her bed. Then, the picture disappeared completely. The chanting faded suddenly with a strangled choke, and all they could hear was Father Romero bellowing up prayers to God. But soon, even his voice faded away.

Angela leaned forward and slapped the monitor, wondering if it was just a technical problem. Liam grabbed her wrist to stop her from hitting it again. "What's going on?" Angela asked.

"I don't know," Liam said as he began pressing buttons on the monitor and fiddling with wires. Without warning, the monitor flashed a bright blue, and then there was a pop of electricity. A thin wisp of smoke twirled upwards from the monitor as if it too had seen too much and wanted nothing to do with the happenings in the house.

Angela flinched as a voice screamed loudly, sounding as if it were coming from everywhere and nowhere at once. She knew that voice. It was Maddie. She leaped from her chair in the kitchen and ran up the stairs, Liam close on her heels.

As she reached the second floor, she saw Scott sitting up and rubbing the back of his head. He looked at his hand to see blood on his fingertips. He forgot about it quickly as he realized that all had gone quiet in Maddie's room. He rose shakily to his feet and tried the doorknob once more. It still did not budge.

"Maddie!" Scott yelled as he tried to force the door open. To Angela he seemed like an animal with one leg caught in a trap, panicked, frantic, ready to break his own body to get away. He threw his shoulder into the door so hard that she winced.

Down the hallway, a door creaked open, and Clayton poked his head out to see what all the noise was about, even though Angela had already told him that under no circumstances was he to open the door.

"Daddy!" Clayton yelled with fear on his face, his eyes as large as plums.

Scott didn't even spare his son a glance. He yelled over his shoulder in a voice that Clayton had never heard before, but which would haunt him the rest of his life. "Go back to bed, Clayton!"

With a squeak, her son disappeared and slammed the door closed.

Scott banged on the door like a madman, while all Angela could think to do was stand in the hallway like an idiot. By the time Scott gave up, sweat poured from his brow and ran down the back of his neck, mixing with his own blood.

Angela was frightened. For all of Scott's banging, there hadn't been a single noise from Maddie's room since her scream. She clutched her hands to her chest, trying not to start crying.

Scott walked away from the door like a beaten man. His eyes were distant, far away. All he could see was the problem before him. "I'm getting my hatchet," he said.

As he strode past Angela, she reached out and grabbed his arm. He turned to look at her as if she had just appeared out of thin air. Angela didn't even recognize him at that moment. She pointed at the door, and he turned to see that the door handle was moving up and down, slowly, as if someone were trying to open the door from within without being heard.

Despite her own heartbeat in her ears and the heavy breathing of Scott, she heard the click of the door's latch. The door edged opened slowly with a small creak, revealing only a small wedge of pitch black.

Angela, Liam, and Scott all shared a look. "Maddie?" Angela called, daring to hope for a response, of which there was none.

They approached the door with fear in their hearts. They knew what they had seen on the monitor. They knew that there was something in the room, or at least, there had been something in the room. Fear gripped their hearts, but somehow, they were able to make themselves enter Maddie's room. For Angela and Scott, it was the love of their daughter that carried them over the threshold. For Liam, it was his scientific curiosity.

Angela reached over to try the light switch. She flipped it up and down, but the darkness remained. A faint haze of smoke hung in the air. The smell of spoiled meat clung to the haze. The candles were all out, but the scent of the smoke from their extinguished wicks was still there, under the spoiled meat smell.

Liam pulled his cell phone from his pocket and turned on the flashlight. He licked his bottom lip as he shined it around the room. His first concern was Maddie, so he shined the flashlight at her bed. Maddie lay there, comatose, her eyes closed. She didn't move at all, but they could see her chest rising and falling.

Angela and Scott rushed over to their daughter.

"Oh, baby. I'm so sorry," Angela said, her voice pitiful and quavering.

Liam turned away from the parents and their emotional display. He aimed his flashlight in another direction.

"Oh, no," Liam said.

"What is it?" Scott asked.

Liam swallowed, a surprisingly hard thing to do at that moment, and said, "It's Matt." The Satanist was curled into a ball on the floor, his hands locked into claws. His eyes were open, as was his mouth, as if he had died mid-scream. Drops of red leaked from the corners of his eyes, as if he had been crying blood.

Liam bent down and placed his fingers to the man's throat. He pressed deeper, hoping to find a faint pulse, something, but he knew it was useless. He began to sweat. His cure was no longer an experiment. It was reality, and now he had cost a man his life. What good was a cure if it cost a life? The medical community would never go for such a thing. But, no, no, maybe this was just part of the learning curve. Maybe the next time he would be ready, more prepared.

"He's in Hell now, where we all will be shortly," Father Romero said from the doorway. He was just a dark shadow, backlit by the light from the hallway. Liam shivered at his words. He didn't believe in heaven or hell, but something in the man's words gave him the creeps.

Father Romero turned then, his head down. Liam watched him walk down the hallway and disappear down the stairs, his mind trying to quantify everything that had happened so far.

****

Scott sat in the living room, feeling like he was living a lie. Behind the police officer, two paramedics wheeled away Matt's body. It was covered, but Scott could still see that face, that screaming damned face. Despite what had happened, he had bigger things to worry about. Right now, there was a police officer staring at him as if he were out of his ever-loving mind.

"Listen, I know this has been a tough night, but the story you all are telling me is ridiculous. What really happened here?" the officer asked.

Scott shook his head. For a moment, they had considered coming up with a story. He, Angela, and Liam had gathered in the living room and started fabricating a lie, when Father Romero came in. He was calm, but Scott could sense the fury within.

"You will not lie about this," Father Romero commanded. "You did nothing wrong, not by the name of the law anyway. To lie about this would be a sin. Stand up and be accountable."

It was almost a relief to hear the words from Father Romero. On top of that, the lie they had come up with wouldn't have fooled a five-year-old. "I told you the truth," Scott said, happy to be able to look the police officer right in the eye. "We all told you the truth."

The cop's mouth fell open, and he looked at Scott with a dead look in his eye. "He summoned a demon and died?"

He had been over the story five times with the police officer now. If he didn't believe him now, there was nothing he could ever do to make him believe. "I know it sounds preposterous, but we're telling the truth. You want to hook me up to a polygraph? I'll do it. We all will. What more do you need?"

But all the police officer did was shake his head, still unable to believe the crazy story that Scott and the others had told him. "We just might take you up on that polygraph." The police officer tucked away his notepad in a pocket and turned to leave the house. At the threshold of the house, he paused and turned back, looking over his shoulder. "Do me a favor."

"Yeah?" Scott replied.

"Stay local. We may have some follow-up questions after the autopsy." He turned and left Scott sitting in the living room, worried about what the autopsy would find. Surely there was nothing there that could implicate any of them.

He pushed the trouble to the back of his mind and ran up the stairs, taking them two at a time. He rushed down the hallway, hoping that Clayton had finally fallen asleep. They had forbidden him from leaving his room, and at this point, he was probably feeling like a prisoner, but it had to be done. He couldn't have his son looking at a dead body.

As he entered Maddie's room, Liam was removing a stethoscope from his ears. His face offered no clue as to the state of Maddie. Angela and Father Romero stood in the room watching the proceedings. Angela nibbled on her thumbnail, a sign that she was feeling nervous.

"Well?" she asked.

"She seems stable," Liam said. "Strong heartbeat, her breathing is fine. Everything seems ok for now."

Angela let out a deep sigh, "Oh good." She said it as if she had expected anything other than good news. Scott himself felt the tension ease, until Father Romero spoke.

"A doctor can't check the soul."

Liam looked at Father Romero with a quizzical look in his eyes. "Can you?" he shot back.

Father Romero said nothing, but the glare he gave Liam wiped the smug smirk off of his face.

"What did the police officer say?" Angela asked.

"It's not good. He told me not to go on vacation. He seems to think we had something to do with Matt's death."

"Maybe we shouldn't have told him the truth," Angela said.

Father Romero said, "You could have told him the real truth. You could have told him that you are responsible for that man's death."

Scott felt his jaw clenching, and it took all of his strength not to lay into Father Romero. "I had nothing to do with it. He was here willingly." He knew his words were only partly true, but he wanted to believe them completely.

"Scott, don't," Angela said trying to calm him down.

But he wouldn't be calmed down. Maybe it was everything that had happened that night, maybe it was the fact that his daughter was still seemingly on death's door, but he had taken enough of Father Romero's holier than thou act. "No, I want to know, Father. Why are you here? If all you're going to do is tell us what we're doing is wrong, then why don't you just leave? I can do a perfectly fine job of telling myself that what we're doing is wrong without you adding your two cents every five minutes."

Father Romero looked at him, bewildered by his outburst. "Why... I'm here to help," he stammered as if it were the most obvious answer in the world.

"Well, then start acting like it," Scott spit, unable to hide the anger in his voice. He wanted the priest to fight, he wanted him to rant and rail, most of all he just wanted to scream at the man.

But Father Romero only nodded his head. "Yes. I'm sorry. It's clear that you know where I stand on all of this." He waved his head to encompass the room, "I suppose I could try a more positive approach to the situation."

And with those reasonable words, Father Romero robbed Scott of his anger, leaving Scott feeling like a deflated balloon. "That would be appreciated," was all he could think to say.

"What do we do now?" Angela asked, quick to move on.

"Now we wait," Liam said.

Chapter 8: The Wait

Liam took a sip of coffee, smacking his lips. He hoped the caffeine would do its trick. Exhaustion had him feeling disconnected from his body. The ritual, the death. So much had happened over the last few hours, but there was so much more to do. But at the moment, he was trying to see if he could fix the video camera he had borrowed from the university. It had stopped working for some reason during the ritual. Renting all of the medical equipment had tapped his resources. If he couldn't fix the video camera, he would be on the hook for the bill, and he knew he was already going to be charged for the monitor, which was shorted out beyond repair.

He wasn't alone in the kitchen. Father Romero sat at the kitchen table, regarding him with some suspicion. "Can I ask you a question, Mr. Brewster?"

The last thing Liam wanted to do was answer any of the priest's questions. Right now, he just wanted to be left alone so that he could fix the camera. "I suppose so," he said, his curiosity getting the better of him. He twisted something within the camera's inner workings, and tightened all of the tiny screws he could find. He was not an electrician, but he crossed his fingers that it would do something.

"How is it possible, with what you have seen tonight, that you do not believe in God?"

Liam considered the priest's question for a moment, then took a sip of bitter coffee. He smacked his lips again and returned to fiddling with the camera. "I believe in faith, Father Romero. Not my own, but in the faith of others. I believe that whatever is happening here is a construct of faith."

"You believe faith made the devil?"

Liam shook his head. "I believe that the human mind, when suitably honed, is capable of manifesting another reality other than the one logical human beings dwell in."

"So Matt's death, the demon in that monitor... it's all been created by our minds?" Father Romero laughed then, setting his own cup of coffee down on the table. "You have way too much faith in the power of humanity, Dr. Bewster."

Liam smiled and said, "It is my religion, you could say." He was proud of his joke. He couldn't remember the last time he had made one. He was only slightly disappointed that Father Romero didn't laugh.

"And what if you're wrong?" Father Romero asked, leaning in conspiratorially.

"If I were wrong, there wouldn't be a little girl lying in her bed dying of cancer in the first place."

"That is..."

"God's plan?" Liam interrupted. He had heard that nonsense before. "Spare me. If God's plan is suffering and death, why would anyone bother worshipping him in the first place?"

"We would bother, as you so bluntly put it, because things can be so much worse. That demon we saw isn't some figment of our imagination. It's there. It's real, and it's our faith in God that keeps the demons at bay." Father Romero paused to take a sip from his coffee, then began again, "And I believe you're about to see that for yourself."

Liam shrugged his shoulders and went back to tinkering on the camera. The truth was, he didn't know what to expect. He didn't know if the priest was right or wrong. Not knowing bothered him, made him nervous. Trying to fix the camera helped. It also kept him from thinking about the death of Matt. The terrified face of Matt's corpse flashed in his mind, and he looked for another screw to tighten, to try and trick the image into going away.

****

Scott slumped in a chair next to Maddie's bed. Angela noted the bags under his eyes. He looked exhausted. Angela knew she must look the same. So much had happened already, and, if Liam was right, worse was in store. *Christ, a man had already died, and there was worse in store. What would the police officer tell Matt's family? Did he have a family, a daughter of his own somewhere?*

"Why don't you go and grab some sleep. One of us should get some rest," Angela suggested.

"I'm not tired," Scott said, and Angela was reminded once again from whom Clayton had inherited his stubborn steak. But she could see Scott was tired. He could barely keep his eyes open.

"Honey, you look exhausted. Go get some rest. I'll come get you if she wakes up."

"Do you promise?"

He must be tired to even ask her that question. "Yeah, we'll take shifts. She'll never be alone." She pulled the life alert necklace from around her neck and handed it to Scott. "Here, take this. If anything happens, you'll know about it."

Scott rose from his chair and shambled over to her. He took the necklace from her outstretched hand and threw it on over his head. He stretched, groaning in pleasant pain, and then leaned down and gave her a peck on the cheek. "If anything happens, I don't care how small, you come and get me. Ok?"

"Got it," she said reassuringly.

She watched him leave, stumbling like an adult version of Clayton when he was exhausted. It was still amazing to her how similar the two were. She always looked for similarities between herself and Maddie, but except for her smile and her hair, when it was healthy and long, there weren't many similarities between herself and her daughter.

She spent time memorizing Maddie's face, every angle, every curve. Hours passed this way. Then, when she was sure she had her daughter's face committed to memory, she picked up the book she had brought to pass the time. She opened the cover of *Candide,* but she didn't even get four pages into her favorite book before her eyelids grew heavy.

****

Clayton had tried to sleep. He had tried to be a good boy, but he couldn't. His head still swam from everything he had heard in his room. The booming voice, the shouting, the police sirens, he was scared out of his mind, but more than that he was curious, so curious. He heard his father stomp past his room. He always knew where Daddy was at any time in the house; his thunderous steps made the upstairs floor quake. But Clayton knew how to be quiet. Clayton knew how to be sneaky. You walked on your toes, never letting your heels touch the floor.

He knew there were other people in the house, that Liam guy, Father Romero, but he also knew the risk was worth it. Something was going on out there, and he couldn't lie in his bed wondering any longer. He weighed the pros and cons of discovery and punishment. He could find out what was going on, or he could be sent to his room with a stern talking to. Either way, he was tired of sitting around.

The boy stalked over to the door and put his hand on the handle. He pressed it down slowly, ever so slowly, his heart beating in his ears. Then, when the handle would go no lower, he opened the door inch by inch. When the opening was large enough to get his head through, he poked his head into the hallway and searched left and then right. He was not sure which direction was left and which was right, but he would figure it out one day.

The hall was empty and dark. He didn't care for the darkness, but at the end of the hallway to his left, or maybe it was his right, he saw a light on in Maddie's room. That was where all the noise had been coming from. Clayton inched the door open wider, until he could slip his whole body into the hallway, and then he stalked down the hallway in his socks. Socks kept footsteps quiet. Through his socks, the floor felt cold on his feet. He was surprised that he could see his breath in front of his face as a quick cloud that disappeared into the air.

In Maddie's room, he found his mother sitting in a chair, her head lolling to the side. A book fell from her hands and hit the floor. He froze, wondering if his mother would wake up at the noise. Her head lolled farther to the side, and then she was still. With his eyes wide in fear, and his heart pumping loudly in his ears, he inched towards Mommy, thinking of how great he was at being sneaky. He leaned down and picked up the book. Briefly he looked inside, but there were too many words for him to want to bother with it. Then, in a stroke of pure audacity, he decided to place the book in Mommy's lap. Slowly, he guided the book towards her hand, a twisted little smile on his face. He was having fun being sneaky. He set the book on her hand, fighting a burst of nearly uncontrollable laughter. It was almost too much to handle.

Then he heard whispering behind him. His head whipped around, and his merriment turned into cold fear. He saw Maddie lying in her bed, her lips moving ever so softly. Her eyes were open, red-veined and terrifying.

"Huh?" he asked his big sister.

"Come here," she whispered, beckoning him with a hooked finger. He hesitated because of the eyes. Those weren't Maddie's eyes. Those eyes were scary. As another breath of cloudy air escaped his lungs, he thought of running back to his room and slamming the door shut. "I have a secret to tell you," she said. Clayton didn't really want to hear Maddie's secret, but he did as she asked because she was his sister, and she was older, and he really didn't want Mommy to wake up and find him out of bed.

He stepped over to Maddie slowly, sure that, at any second, Mommy was going to wake up and yell at him. He almost wished she would. As he came nearer, Maddie moved herself to a sitting position, though the movement seemed difficult for her. She leaned over, and Clayton turned his head so she could speak into his ear.

He didn't see her lips as they moved impossibly fast, but his eyes grew larger and larger with each syllable. His eyes filled with tears, but only a faint whispering filled the room. Her lips flew faster, and Clayton didn't like what he heard, not at all. He wished he could walk away, but he felt stuck. His feet wouldn't move though he desperately wanted them to. Her voice changed in his ear, morphing from the sweet voice of his sister to something darker. He was sure that if he turned his head, he would not see his sister anymore. He would see something else, a monster, a creature, maybe something with horns. That's what the monsters always had in his dreams.

When she was done speaking, Maddie lay down and went back to sleep. He ran from the room, not caring if Mommy or Daddy heard him.

****

Scott woke up feeling like shit. His body ached. The first thing he noticed was the smell. At first, he thought it was his own stench, but then he realized it was the same smell that had been carried on the wind that knocked him into the door last night. He sat up in the bed, his head aching. He reached up and touched the spot where his head had crashed into the door and then pulled his fingers away quickly, wincing. He had quite a knot back there.

He stood then, and memories of the night came flooding back into him. He felt his blood begin to pump, and he popped out of bed, clutching his head as he did so. His head pounded. It was like the worst hangover he had ever had times ten. He walked down the hallway, noting the quiet of the house. He clutched at the life alert necklace that hung around his neck, though it was silent.

In Maddie's room, he found everything as he had left it. Maddie slept in her bed, the oxygen mask still on her face. Angela's head was thrown backward, her body slumped in the chair where he had left her, her book on the floor. Judging from the position she was sleeping in, she was going to wake up as sore as he was, but he decided to let her sleep. She needed it. He took a deep breath, noting the smell again. *Something rotten,* he thought. *Maybe a mouse died somewhere. Hopefully not in the walls, or they'd never find the source of the smell.*

From the hallway behind him, he heard a faint sound. It sounded like sobbing. He turned around, forgetting the smell for a moment, and walked back into the hallway. He stood there, his head cocked to the side, listening for the sound. There it was again. It was definitely the sound of sobbing. Clayton.

He opened the door to Clayton's room and stepped inside. He hissed in pain as he stepped on one of Clayton's many action figures. Iron Man. He kicked it to the side in anger, and then he heard the sobbing, a little louder this time, but still muffled. It came from the closet.

The door to the closet was open just a crack. Scott walked over and pulled the door open to find Clayton sitting on the floor, his knees pulled up to his chest, tears running down his cheeks. Concerned, Scott squatted down to get a better look at the boy. *Was he hurt?* "Hey, buddy. What's going on?" he asked in a soothing voice.

Clayton didn't respond. He just buried his face between his drawn-up knees and continued his crying. "Talk to me, buddy." Scott put a hand out and rubbed Clayton's back.

Clayton lifted his head up, his face red and covered in tears and snot. *How long has he been in here crying?*

His son wiped his face with his arm and looked up at him with red eyes. In halting, gasping words, he said, "Maddie said we're all going to burn in hell." Then he continued crying some more.

Scott sat back on his heels, his mind running in twenty different directions at once. Maddie talking? "What do you mean 'Maddie said?' Did you have a nightmare?" That was the only explanation Scott could think of.

"No. I wasn't dreaming, Dad," Clayton wailed, pausing for a gulp of air. "She said it last night."

That doesn't make sense. If Maddie had woken up, they would have known it. "When last night?"

"The light was on in her room, and I just wanted to see her, and she was awake." He paused to snort in snot and wipe his face with his arm. "And I went in there, and she was awake, and she whispered in my ear." He began sobbing again. More tears ran down his cheeks. Scott rubbed his back again, trying to get him to calm down, and then Clayton said, "She said bad things, Daddy." He began to wail even louder.

Scott pulled Clayton to him, encircling the boy in his arms. "It's ok. She's just sick. She's going to be alright." He didn't know if Clayton was telling the truth. He didn't see how anything he said could have happened, but that didn't matter. At that moment, he just wanted to let Clayton know that everything was going to be fine.

"She said that you and Mommy don't love me. Is that true?"

Scott looked down at his son, shock on his face. "No. There could be nothing further from the truth. We both love you. I'd do anything for you."

"She said that I should just kill myself."

Scott had no answer for that one, so he just pulled Clayton closer and hugged him to his chest. They sat that way for a long time, and when Clayton had stopped crying, he laid him down in his bed and pulled the covers over him. When he went to leave, Clayton reached out a small hand and wouldn't let him go. So he stayed until Clayton drifted off to sleep.

****

Scott pulled open the front door to find Gael standing there. She had volunteered to babysit Clayton until everything with Maddie was done. He still didn't know if he believed Clayton's story, but he knew that something had scared the shit out of him the night before. Regardless, he and Angela had both agreed that the house was no place for him to be. Let him spend time with Gael, watching superhero movies and eating ice cream for dinner.

Without asking, she wrapped her arms around him and gave him a hug. Angela had told her everything. Scott let the hug happen. It felt right. Though he and Gael had never been particularly close, he had a great respect for her, and dammit, at that moment, they could all use a hug.

When she stopped hugging him, he bent down and lifted up a suitcase. "I've packed Clayton's things here. Thanks for taking him."

"It's no problem, really. How long do you think until..." Gael couldn't finish saying the words. "How long do you think it will be?"

"I don't know," he answered honestly.

Angela rounded the corner with Clayton at her hip. "Come on, Clayton. You're going to have a great time with

Gael, and when you get back, Maddie will be all better and we'll have a feast, and you'll get to eat whatever you want."

Angela was throwing out a lot of promises, but with God's grace, they would be able to meet every single one of them.

Clayton looked at Angela with hope in his eyes. "Ice cream?"

"Yep," Angela said.

"Cake?" he asked, testing his limits.

"Whatever you can think of," Angela replied.

"Should you really be saying that stuff about Maddie?" Gael asked. She had a point, but Scott didn't think this was the time or place to bring it up.

Angela said, "She's going to get better, Gael. I know it."

Gael looked Angela in the eyes for a moment, and then, seeing that Angela meant every word she said, she let it drop. She bent down and grabbed Clayton's hand in her own wrinkled one. "Well, keep your hopes high and your expectations low, that's what I always say."

"We're doing our best here, Gael."

Gael gave Angela a disapproving look, but then she looked at Clayton, a grandmotherly smile spreading across her face. She squatted down until she was at eye level with Clayton. "Are you ready to come spend some time with me?"

Clayton nodded, last night's scare still plain on his face.

"Alright, Let's go."

Clayton turned to his mother then and said, "Maddie is evil, Mommy. Stay away from her."

All of the adults shared a look, but Clayton just turned to Gael and held out his hand. She grabbed it and said, "Come on, Clayton. Let's go to my house." With her other hand, she picked up Clayton's tiny suitcase, and together they toddled off to Gael's car. Scott and Angela waved at Clayton as he left, but he did not wave back.

****

Light, pure and golden, poured into Maddie's room in stark contrast to Angela's mood. She stood drinking a cup of coffee, trying to keep herself alert as she stared at Maddie's still form. She kept going through Clayton's story in her mind. She spoke to him... Maddie spoke. It seemed like the stuff of nightmares. She knew Clayton was sensitive. Maybe all the goings-ons in the house had gotten to him.

She looked at Maddie. Nothing had changed. She began to wonder if perhaps she had imagined it all. The wind, the voices, the image on the monitor... nothing seemed different, not that she could see anyway. But she felt something. She felt a sort of shift, and the logical part of her mind wanted her to dismiss is as just her imagination. But she couldn't change what she felt.

Liam moved about the bed, checking the readouts on the equipment. He checked to see that the electrodes and wires were hooked up correctly.

"Do you believe what Clayton said?" she asked him.

He eyed her speculatively out of the corner of his eye. He obviously didn't like to be disturbed while he was working. "You know better than I do. Does he frequently make up stories like that?"

She thought about it. Clayton was many things, but he wasn't a liar. He was a hider. He would just as soon not tell you something, but when called out on it, he would always own up to what he had done whether that be drawing on the wall in markers or knocking things over on the counter in his quest to find where the cookies were hidden. "I don't think Clayton has learned how to lie... yet." All children learned to lie sooner or later.

"Then maybe it was like Scott said. Just a dream. Perhaps all the commotion last night got to the boy."

His thoughts mirrored her own, but the answer still didn't sit right with her. "What about your friend Matt? Was that a dream too?"

"He wasn't my friend. And I'm sure once the coroner's report comes back, there will be a perfectly natural explanation for his... er... demise." Liam bent down and tucked his hands underneath Maddie's back. "Would you like to give me a hand here? I'd like to get a sample of her spinal fluid."

Angela set her coffee cup down on the nightstand next to Maddie's bed. She leaned across the bed, and between her and Liam, they managed to roll her over on her side. Liam grabbed a large syringe, larger than any Angela had ever seen outside of a joke Halloween costume. He positioned the syringe against Maddie's spine.

"Do you know what you're doing with that?" she asked.

Liam looked at her and licked his lower lip. "Yes," he said simply.

Angela refused to turn away, though she had never been a huge fan of needles. If she had stopped to look at Maddie's face during the procedure, she would have seen Maddie lying there with her eyes open, a peculiar smile on her face.

But she did notice when Maddie's hand darted out, grabbed her cup of coffee and flung the scalding liquid at Angela. She screamed in pain, slapping at the coffee like her body was covered in flames.

"Maddie, you're awake," she managed to say as she pulled her wet shirt away from her body.

Maddie laughed, a haunting sound, dry as fall leaves skittering across pavement.

"Why did you do that, Maddie? It burned."

Liam just stood with the syringe in his hands, his eyes big, his wet, lower lip quivering as if he were trying to say something.

Maddie hissed at Angela.

"Maddie, is that you?" Liam finally managed to ask.

The girl on the bed turned towards him, ripping the I.V. from her arm. A squirt of blood jetted onto the blue sheets. "Get out of my room, liar."

Angela moved towards Maddie. She didn't know what was wrong, but her daughter was alive and talking. "Are you feeling alright, dear?"

"Don't go near her. That's not your little girl anymore, Angela." It was Father Romero. She didn't know when he had come into the room, but now he was standing in the door. Angela looked at him, confused. Then Maddie laughed again, and the hair on Angela's arms stood on end. She didn't understand her own reaction to her daughter's laughter. This was Maddie, the child she gave birth to, but why did it feel so wrong?

"Don't be ridiculous. She's just ill." *That has to be why she's acting like this.*

Maddie ripped the electrodes off her body and threw the oxygen mask onto the floor.

"No, don't take those off," Liam said, moving towards her to pick up the mask.

"But I'm feeling much better," the girl on the bed stated.

Father Romero strode toward Maddie, and she recoiled in fear. "Hold your filthy tongue," he commanded. Father Romero took her by the shoulders and pushed her back onto the bed.

Liam rushed to pull Father Romero off of her. "Leave her alone!" Liam shouted as Scott hurried into the room, the life alert necklace beeping around his neck.

Maddie saw Scott over Father Romero's shoulder, and for the first time she spoke in a voice that Angela recognized. "Help me, Daddy. He's going to hurt me."

"Get your hands off of her!" Scott shouted over the noise of the necklace.

Father Romero ignored Scott, shrugged off Liam, and attempted to restrain Maddie once again. "Don't you see what she is?" he asked.

"That's my little girl," Scott said.

"Maybe she's in there somewhere, but this is not your little girl! You should be helping me!" While Father Romero's attention was diverted, Maddie lashed out at him with a free hand, tearing three bloody scratches on his cheek. Then, in a voice that sounded nothing like Maddie, she said, "He said get your goddamn hands off me."

Father Romero backed away from Maddie, putting his hand to his cheek. His fingertips came away bloody.

Angela couldn't make sense of what was happening. She watched in disbelief as her daughter sat up in bed and hopped into a squatting position, ready to pounce. Her fingernails were longer than Angela remembered. She had just trimmed them the other day. Her eyes were red, as if her pupils swam in blood. Maddie began shredding her own skin with those long fingernails. First her arm, then her face, digging long, bloody furrows.

"No!" Angela wailed feeling the pain of Maddie's self-inflicted wounds, though Maddie didn't seem to care.

Then Maddie began digging at the skin on her chest, tearing her nightgown to shreds with those long fingernails. "I want to see my heart," she crooned in her demented voice, the voice that Angela was sure didn't belong to Maddie... it belonged to whatever was inside her daughter.

Angela, knowing that she wasn't talking to her daughter, but not sure what else to do said, "Stop it, Maddie! You're hurting yourself."

Liam backed away and thumped against the wall, as far away from Maddie as he could get, his eyes wide.

Father Romero ran his hand through his silver hair and said, "Help me tie her down before she does any more harm to herself." And it suddenly struck Angela that maybe they should have listened to Father Romero in the first place... about everything. Father Romero rushed at Maddie, slapping her clawing hands to the side. Angela rushed in as well, and she was glad to see Scott joining them. Over her shoulder, she saw Liam shrinking against the wall, his mouth open in awe.

Maddie lashed out with her hands and sent Father Romero sprawling to the floor. Angela attempted to wrestle her daughter's arms to her side, but she felt like she was the child and Maddie was the adult while grappling with her daughter. She didn't know where Maddie's strength came from, but it was not the normal strength of a teenage girl, especially not one who had been sick with cancer for months.

Her daughter's mouth opened, exposing a blackened tongue, and from the depths of her lungs, she let loose a blood-curdling scream. The sound physically hurt Angela, driving into her brain, and she shrunk away from Maddie, her ears ringing. She put her hands to her ears, and watched the flesh of Maddie's cheeks flap with the force of her scream. What was left of her hair floated upward, and black blood began to seep from the wounds that she had created.

Maddie waved a hand, and Father Romero's sprawled body went sliding out of the room and into the hallway. The girl on the bed raised her hand and made a fist. The door slammed shut.

She had to do something. Angela didn't know what she could do, but she had to do something. This was already out of control, and she didn't want the situation to escalate any further. "Baby, are you in there?"

The creature on the bed looked at her, as if she were insignificant. "She's not here. She's burning in the cold flames of hell. Thanks, Mom."

While the creature was focused on her, Angela saw Liam sneaking up behind her. Scott must have seen him as well because, in order to keep their daughter's attention focused on them, he said, "We want our daughter back."

The creature on the bed smiled, exposing rotten teeth, "There's only one way to see her now." She paused, seeming on the verge of laughter. "You must die." Maddie flung her arm in an arc away from her body, and Scott went flying through the air to slam into the wall. His arms went limp and he slid to the floor, unconscious.

Behind Maddie, Liam leaped at the bed, wrapping his arms around the child. Angela didn't hesitate this time; she jumped as quick as she could, wrestling with Maddie, trying to prevent her from getting her arms free.

Outside the room, Angela heard Father Romero banging on the door trying to get inside. Angela's eyes went wide as the room began to quake. Bits of plaster filtered down from the ceiling. "Unhand me," the creature commanded, for it was a creature; Angela knew that now. Whatever was inside her daughter, it was not Maddie, and she knew that she couldn't listen to it. "Unhand me, worm." But she didn't release her hold on Maddie. She couldn't because she didn't know what the creature would do to Maddie's body, what it had already done. She saw the scratches and claw marks in her baby's flesh, and she wanted to cry.

"Get something to tie her up with!" Liam yelled. Maddie spat at him. The spittle landed on his cheek, where it began to sizzle. He screamed in pain, turning his head from side to side as Maddie strained against him.

Angela released her hold on Maddie, hoping that the young man was strong enough to keep Maddie in check. Angela pulled the sheets from the bed like a magician tugging a tablecloth out from underneath a set table. She tied one end of the sheet to Maddie's left foot. She quickly began knotting the other end around the metal railing at the foot of the bed, as Maddie thrashed and bucked trying to dislodge Liam's hold.

Scott woke up then, his hands going to his head. He groaned in pain, rolled to his side and then pushed himself to his feet shakily. He saw Angela tying Maddie's foot to the bed, and with his eyes squinting from the pain, he staggered to the closet. He threw the door open and pulled out an old jump rope of Maddie's. He stumbled over to the bed and began tying up Maddie's other foot.

Outside the room, Angela could hear Father Romero bellowing and slamming on the door as she finished tying her knot. Suddenly, the door fell inward, and Father Romero appeared with a hammer in his hand. He had removed the pins from the door's hinges.

The creature on the bed locked eyes with Angela and began to growl. The growl deepened and swelled, louder and louder, building to a point where Angela began to feel the inside of her own skull vibrate. The window in Maddie's room shattered inward, spraying everyone with glass. Father Romero got the worst of it. He dropped the hammer to the ground and threw his hands over his face to protect himself. A cold fog blew into the room.

"Talk to her, Angela! She'll listen to you," Father Romero yelled over the howl of wind and the growling of Maddie.

Angela heard him, but she didn't know what to say. She opened her mouth, and the words came pouring out. "Baby, if you're in there, I need you to fight. I know you've been fighting for so long, but I need you to keep going."

The wind howled louder, bits of broken glass sliding across the wooden floor. Maddie convulsed on the bed, her back arching, her head thrown back. It was all Liam could do just to hold on.

Maybe this is Maddie fighting. Maybe my little girl's still in there somewhere. "We need you here with us! So fight, dammit! Fight!"

Maddie screamed in pain. Her back arched, her face covered in sweat. Suddenly, she stopped struggling, the life draining out of her. Maddie collapsed on the bed, and Liam dove on top of her. Her chest heaved as if she had just finished a marathon. The room was calm and quiet, but Angela's ears still rang from Maddie's assault. The curtains to Maddie's window slowly fluttered back to their resting position. Slowly, Maddie's eyes opened.

She looked around the room, her neck barely able to hold up her head. "Mommy? Daddy? What are you doing?"

Angela's hands went to her mouth. That was her voice. That was her little girl speaking. Her eyes were clear, not the bloodshot stuff of nightmares.

"Don't just stand there, Father," Liam said, gasping for breath on Maddie's chest with a death grip on her arms. "Get something to tie her hands."

"There's rope in the garage," Scott said absentmindedly as he approached Maddie's bed. Father Romero rushed from the room.

"What's going on?" Maddie asked. "You guys are scaring me."

Angela walked to the bed as well, searching for the words to say. But there was nothing that she could tell her daughter. How could you tell someone you loved that you had just put a... a demon inside her? Maddie began to cry, and Angela put a hand to her head, brushing the few pitiful, sweat-soaked strands of hair back from her forehead.

"It's alright, baby. You're going to be just fine." *She had to be. For any of this to be worth it, she just had to be.*

Her daughter's breathing slowed, and she was still confused. "What's going on? I was having the worst nightmares. It was dark. And I wanted to scream, but every time I opened my mouth, another voice came out."

Father Romero rushed back into the room, rope held in his hands. Without ceremony, he grabbed Maddie's arm and began tying it to one of the metal rails of the bed.

"Father Romero?" Maddie asked, her eyes going from his face to her arm and back to his face again. Father Romero ignored her, tying the knot as tight as he could without cutting off the circulation.

"Is this really necessary?" Angela asked. She didn't like seeing her daughter trussed up like a Thanksgiving turkey.

"Why?" Maddie asked Father Romero, her voice pitiful enough to bring tears to Angela's eyes.

"It's for your own good, child," Father Romero responded.

"Just rest, dear," Angela said, stroking Maddie's head. It was all she could think to say.

"You must be strong, Maddie. You must be as strong as you have ever been," Father Romero said.

"Am I dying?" she asked.

Scott finished tying off Maddie's other arm with the last of the rope, and Liam finally climbed off of Maddie's torso. He adjusted his glasses and wiped at the burn on his cheek with the back of his hand. "That's why we're all here, Maddie. To keep that from happening."

Scott leaned in and kissed Maddie on the forehead. "It's gonna be ok," he said. Maddie squeezed her eyes shut, and tears rolled down her cheeks.

Scott's words played over and over in Angela's mind. *It's gonna be ok.* But was it? Was it really?

****

Maddie slept in her bed, her chest rising and falling. Liam had reattached the leads of the machines and placed the oxygen mask back on her face. The steady beep of the EKG machine was the only sound in the room.

Scott and Maddie sat in their chairs, watching, waiting for Maddie to wake up again. Scott couldn't believe it. He couldn't believe the horror of the situation. He couldn't believe that the spark of hope in his chest was now in full bloom. They had brought her back! She had spoken to them, heard their voices, recognized their faces.

Yet, every time he let the hope rise, a tiny voice in the back of his head asked, "But yes, at what cost?" At what cost indeed? They hadn't told Maddie what was going on. They were too happy simply to talk to her, to let her know that everything was going to be ok. They hadn't told her exactly how she was going to be ok. Maddie was old enough to understand that not everything was right. She was too smart. The questions would come, and he was trying to figure out what to say to his daughter. Would she hate him for this? Would she hold this against him for the rest of her life? But then... without Liam's cure... he let the thought go, and focused on the beeping of the EKG, the rise and fall of his daughter's chest.

Father Romero poked his head into the room, a grim look on his face. But that was nothing new, his face had been grim since he had seen the video of Katie Custary's exorcism. That Father Romero had not called the video out as a sham was not lost on Scott.

"Can I see you both in the kitchen?" he asked.

"But what about Maddie?" Angela asked.

"It will be for just a moment," he reassured her.

Angela looked at Scott, and he shrugged his shoulders. He needed to move around anyway, get his blood flowing. Angela clutched the life alert necklace at her chest as she rose. They followed Father Romero through the house, winding their way past photographs of better times. There would be more times like those, times at the beach, birthday parties, celebrations... maybe even a graduation in the near future. What would Maddie do with her new life?

In the kitchen, Liam was eating a sandwich with one hand while wiping at the burn mark on his cheek with the other. Scott spared him a glance. It might peel, it might blister, but it was too soon to tell if the burn was going to leave a scar on his face.

He and Angela sat at the kitchen table. They had said hardly two words to each other since... the incident. He didn't know what to say. To be quite honest, fear clutched at his chest every time he thought about what she might be thinking. Was she silently cursing him for letting her go through with this? Was she feeling regret for letting Liam Brewster try to cure Maddie? He wanted to ask her, wanted to talk to her and see what was on her mind, but he took the coward's way out. "What's going on, Father?"

"I wanted to talk to you both away from Maddie. She needs her rest, and well, I didn't want what's inside her to hear what I said. I have to say that I'm not happy about the path that you have chosen, but now that we are upon this path, I just wanted to let you know that I will see you through to the end."

For a wonder, it sounded like he actually meant it.

Angela said, "Thank you, Father. That means a lot to us."

Without pausing or acknowledging her words, Father Romero bulled on. "I also wanted you to know that Maddie, or whatever that is in there, is going to get a whole lot worse."

Worse? How could this possibly get any worse? The thought that anything could be worse than what they had already gone through tying Maddie to her bed... he just couldn't wrap his mind around it. "What do you mean, worse?"

Father Romero nodded his head. He had clearly been thinking about how to say what he needed to say at that moment. "I mean, that right now, Maddie is fighting off whatever is inside of her. Right now, she has battled it back, but it will come back again, and in force. Stronger, meaner, more wicked, if you can imagine such a thing."

"Do you have experience with these types of things, Father?" Angela asked.

It struck Scott then, something that had been bothering him ever since Father Romero had watched the video. He knew. He knew about Liam's cure, if not the cure part, he had not flinched at the video of the girl being possessed. He didn't know why he hadn't realized it before.

Father Romero, cleared his throat and rubbed at his neck with his hand, as if trying to massage the words out of his mouth. "It's not something we talk about at the church, or even in public at all, but, yes, I studied this phenomenon at seminary school."

For the first time, Liam seemed to become aware of Scott, Angela, and Father Romero's presence in the kitchen. He perked up and said, "Fascinating. I've tried talking to priests about my theories, but none of them would even acknowledge the existence of demons."

Father Romero shot Liam a withering look. "It's not fascinating, Mr. Brewster. It's terrifying. Right now, their little girl is in there fighting for her soul. In her weakened state, I give her less than a week, and then she'll be gone."

"What do you mean gone?" Scott asked. The priest turned to him and said nothing. "Do you mean dead?"

Liam adjusted his glasses on his face. "No, I don't believe there's a chance of that," he said matter-of-factly.

Scott glared at him, but before he could say anything, Father Romero said, "Mr. Brewster is correct. Maddie's body will continue to live on, but not as Maddie... but as that thing in there. No matter what we do, we'll never be able to bring her back. The devil will have won, and your little girl will have no hope of ever seeing this world again."

"Is this true?" Angela asked Liam, her voice accusatory, containing the barest hint of rage.

Liam shrugged his shoulders. "This is all experimental for me. It could be true."

Scott couldn't believe what he was hearing. Where was the cocky doctor now? Where was the man that had claimed he was 83-percent sure that he could cure their daughter?

Angela, on the verge of a complete breakdown shouted, "Experimental! You said you could save her."

Scott flexed his fists on the kitchen table, opening and closing his hands. He thought he could bash the table to pieces at that moment, and then maybe Liam as well.

Liam went on, unapologetic, "You want me to give you definitive answers, and I can't. You want me to say the odds of saving Maddie are a hundred percent, but I can't say that. I wouldn't say that. But I will say that the percentage is better than zero, which is what Maddie was facing without this treatment."

"Percentages," Scott scoffed, an image of Liam's bloody, beaten face swirling in his mind. "Is that all you have for us?"

Liam looked at Scott then, determination on his face. For only perhaps the third time in the days they had spent together, he made direct eye contact with him, and Scott could sense a burning passion in those eyes. "Percentages... and my word, Mr. Cutter. If there's anything I can do to save your daughter, I will do it."

It was good enough. Scott managed to swallow his anger and unclenched his fists. He stood and walked to the kitchen counter, leaning on its edge and looking out the window. The inflatable pool stood out there, leaves floating on its surface. "If what you two are saying is true, then shouldn't we start trying to get that thing out of her right now?"

Liam shook his head and said, "No, she needs more time."

"More time for what?" Father Romero asked exasperated.

"More time for whatever is inside her to change her physiology. Maddie's cancer was spread throughout her entire body. Whatever is possessing her acts like a parasitic symbiote. It wants to cause damage and pain, but it doesn't want to kill the body. It has already boosted Maddie's immune system. Come. I'll show you."

****

Angela stood holding onto Scott's arm. They watched as Liam threw back Maddie's covers. He gestured at the wounds on one of her arms.

"You can already see how fast she is healing," he said, like a professor giving a presentation, pointing to the scratches on her arms, light pink scars that looked like they had been made some time ago. There wasn't even any evidence of scabbing.

Angela couldn't believe it. But there it was... proof... of something.

"How long until the cancer is gone?" Scott asked, giving Angela's hand a small squeeze.

"That I don't know," Liam said. "If what Father Romero says is true..."

"It's true," Father Romero interrupted.

"Then I would say we need to wait as long as we can. We don't want this to have all been for nothing," Liam said.

Father Romero harrumphed and said, "You just don't want to fail your precious experiment."

Liam readjusted his glasses, and Angela feared that Father Romero and Liam would burst into another argument. But all Liam said was, "I'm not a bad person, you know. I do want to help."

Father Romero indulged Liam and said, "I know you want to help, Mr. Brewster. I don't question that. I just wish that you had considered the spiritual implications of your cure before you decided to go ahead with it."

Liam didn't respond to Father Romero. Instead, he turned his attention to Maddie, chewing on his lower lip in thought. Maddie's chest rose and fell. Her eyes were closed, and her brow wrinkled briefly, as if she were in pain.

Chapter 9: In a Dark Place

Maddie was alive... she knew she was alive, but she didn't know where. The world around her was gloomy, marked by a darkness that seemed to disappear at the edges of her eyes. When she turned to glimpse the brightness, it retreated, as if it were playing hide and seek with her.

She was in an old place... a strange place. She didn't recognize it. Maybe it came from a movie. The walls were made from stone bricks, heavy and yellow. They had the smell of age about them, ancient dust accumulated in all the nooks and crannies. Her bare feet slid across a smooth, cobblestone floor.

Her breath seemed to echo underneath the arched ceiling, where pitch-black shadows seemed to shift like the water in a sun-soaked swimming pool. Anything could be hiding in there, hiding above her, and she didn't know why, but a part of her felt as if she were being watched from the shadowy depths. Outside... she needed to get outside.

She moved through the hallway. Her legs felt sluggish, unused. Her mouth was dry, and as she tried to wet her mouth, it seemed the air itself stole the moisture out of her mouth. "Mom? Dad?" she called. *Surely, they must be here somewhere.* They wouldn't leave her in some mysterious place like this to find her own way out.

The hallway seemed to drag on. Telescoping. That was the word that came to Maddie's mind. Just when she thought she surely must reach the end of the hallway, it seemed to shift, expanding and putting her right back where she had started. Her heart beat heavily in her chest.

She turned to look behind her and screamed. There was something there, something crawling along the hallway, filling it. She had the impression of spines and eyes. If she listened closely, she could hear a soft skittering. It would be upon her in any second. She turned and ran, knowing that it was hopeless to try and escape something with so many legs and arms, if that's what those spiny protrusions were.

Maddie felt like she was on a treadmill. Her mom had owned one of those once upon a time. Though the only time it had ever seemed to see any use was when she and Clayton had turned it on and played on it, dust flying in the air. She had laughed as she turned the treadmill up as high as it would go, and Clayton tried to step onto it, only to lose his balance, fall and be pushed off the edge. But she knew how he felt now. Below her, her feet pounded, but the floor seemed to be working against her. For every step forward, she took one step back. "Mom! Dad!" she screamed.

There was no response. Behind her, she felt cold breath on her neck. Maddie knew that if she turned around, it would all be over, the running, the everything. She pumped her fists, but the shadows grew darker and darker. She could hear the clawing on the walls now. She could hear sounds like words, words that she felt like she should understand, but which she didn't.

"Mom!" she yelled. The voices around her hissed, as if mocking her, or perhaps trying out the words she had said to see how they felt on whatever alien lips they passed. "Dad!" she screamed, and the voices mocked her again. From the corner of her eye, several black shadows entered her field of vision. They were fingers, dark, covered in fur and ending in tips that looked sharp. She ran and ran, her body covered in a cold sweat, but her running did no good. The fingers curled and pressed slowly into the flesh of her shoulder, digging into her flesh. Small streams of blood dripped down her skin.

Immediately, the voices intensified, flooding her mind and blocking out all other senses. They weren't scary voices now; they were inviting voices. "Rest," they purred, and an image of herself curled up and sleeping filled her mind. "Reeeesssttt," they purred again. But she couldn't.

She kept fighting. She slapped at the fingers embedded in her flesh. She called out for help, muttering a prayer that she had used to say as a child. The fingers tensed in her shoulder, and then withdrew from her. She continued to pray and then dropped to her knees, her head spinning, and the world wavering around her as if she were underwater. She didn't look behind her, but she could hear the skittering of legs, maybe hundreds of them, sliding across the brick walls and cobblestone floor of the hallway.

****

Scott flipped the switch for the porchlight. Through the front porch, he saw the front yard. The lawn needed to be mowed, but that was a problem for another day. The streets were quiet, as if the entire neighborhood was waiting for something. He pulled the curtains closed. His entire world was inside the house now, with the exception of Clayton. But Clayton was in a safe place, and that gave him one less thing to worry about, though in truth, he still worried about the boy and whatever Maddie had told him the night before. Maybe it was real... maybe whatever was inside Maddie had actually talked to his son. The thought made him queasy. He was responsible for that, and sooner or later, he would answer for it.

But for now, he needed sleep. Scott was exhausted. Angela was upstairs, keeping an eye on Maddie... if she was still Maddie. He ambled to the living room and flopped on the couch, spreading out his body.

Father Romero sat in the recliner reading from his bible, his lower lip going up and down as he silently mouthed the words to himself. As Scott sighed on the sofa, his spine unwinding from an afternoon of sitting in a chair, Father Romero said, "I would get your sleep while you can. It's going to be a long night."

Scott threw an arm over his eyes, blocking out the orange-tinted light from the lamp on the end table. "Why do you say that?"

"The powers of darkness are always stronger without the sun to hold them at bay."

"What are they?" Scott asked.

Father Romero sighed and said, "The church refers to them as demons, but that's just a catch-all phrase for any number of nasty entities that prey upon the human mind, body, and soul."

Scott had no real reply for Father Romero's answer. It didn't make him feel any better, and it didn't make him feel any less exhausted. "Well, whatever it is, I'll feel better when it's gone."

"Let's just hope we can get rid of it when the time comes."

They lapsed into silence then, Father Romero lost in his bible and Scott trying to fall asleep.

****

Angela hummed a tune to herself as she folded clothes. She didn't want to leave Maddie alone in that room, all by herself. If she woke up, she wanted Maddie to know that someone had been there, someone had been waiting for her to wake. She slid the clothes into the dresser, unaware that behind her, she was being watched.

The creature on the bed had opened Maddie's eyes, allowing it to see into the room. It was still weak, but it was growing in strength. It was gathering what strength it had, but its hunger was almost too much to bear. It had a void inside of it, inside of the girl, and it needed to feed that void... it needed to put something in there, something that only the girl possessed. It had touched what it wanted, but the girl had thrown her back with... the Pact, the contract that had existed between man and demon for thousands of years. Man grew weaker though. They had forgotten many of the ways of the Pact... they could be had. The balance could be undone.

The creature closed the girl's eyes when it sensed Angela's awareness.

When Angela turned around to look at Maddie, she was the same as the last time she had looked, sickly-looking, but still breathing. Angela turned back around to finish the laundry, though her skin was raised in gooseflesh, and she had the oddest sensation of being watched.

The creature opened the girl's eyes once more. It became easier every time. It watched the mother as she did her chores, and it waited. "Soon... Soon..." it growled.

****

Angela and Scott sat at the dining room table, shoveling salad into their mouths. They ate mostly in silence. There was nothing to say. They both felt shame and regret at their actions, but their daughter was alive. They would both do anything for her, though doubt had begun to creep into their minds.

Liam rushed into the room carrying the video camera, his excitement in stark contrast to Scott and Angela's malaise.

"You're supposed to be watching, Maddie," Scott snapped.

Liam didn't seem to notice Scott's anger. Instead, he said, "You guys have to see this." He powered on the camera and angled the viewfinder so they could both watch. Scott and Angela moved shoulder to shoulder to watch as the scene from the previous night played out. "There! Did you see it?" Liam asked triumphantly.

"See what? What are we supposed to be looking for?" Angela asked.

"Here. Let me rewind it." Liam leaned between them and fiddled with the buttons on the viewfinder. He pressed play and the video began, this time going frame by frame. The candles in the room flickered, fading and spiking. Then Angela saw it...a thing... a demon. It had glowing blue eyes and more arms and legs and things in between than her mind could comprehend. Its form was shadowy, almost translucent, like a cloud covered in spines.

"You shouldn't be looking at that," Father Romero said. "It will do you no good."

"What is it, Father?" Angela asked.

"It's evil. That's all, Angela."

Tears came to her eyes. "That thing is in our little girl." *How could I? How could I do this?* She knew she was to blame. If she hadn't kept that card, if she hadn't made that phone call... if she hadn't convinced Scott, none of this would be happening right now.

"We'll get it out. You can get it out, right, Liam?" Scott asked.

"I think I can. I've studied videos," Liam said.

"Studied videos?" Scott asked, bewildered.

Father Romero spoke to Liam, "Without faith, Mr. Brewster, you have zero chance of succeeding. You might as well be asking a spider to write the Bible."

Liam, unperturbed, said, "I have my faith, Father, faith in science."

"Knowing that two plus two equals four is not going to aid you in this instance," Father Romero said.

Liam nodded his head. "What do you propose?"

Father Romero nodded, as if steeling himself. "When the time comes, I will do it."

Relief flooded Angela's body, and a great sigh escaped her lips. Father Romero patted her on the shoulder and said, "But first, I need to go to my church and get a book."

"What type of book?" an intrigued Liam asked.

"It is a book with no name. You see, there are rules. Demons can't just do whatever they want. No, that would be the end of us. They are bound by the will of God, as we all are. I will need it to conduct the ritual if we are to have any chance of banishing the being that inhabits your daughter."

"Oh, please hurry, Father." She wanted to see Father Romero run from the house. She wanted to see him sprint.

But Father Romero did no such thing. He stood in a stately manner and said, "I will be as quick as I can." He exited the kitchen, leaving Liam, Angela, and Scott alone. With the smell of rot lingering in her nose, Angela prayed that he would be back soon.

****

Angela had pulled a chair close to the foot of Maddie's bed. Maddie slept deeply, flinching every now and then as if stuck in an awful nightmare. She sat and she waited, wondering where Father Romero was and how soon he would be back.

She looked at her daughter's face for the thousandth time and tried to envision a future for Maddie, a future where she could run, smile, and laugh. It didn't matter what she did. She could work at Taco Bell or become a politician; all that mattered to Angela was that she would be successful and happy in her life. And if she wasn't successful, then Angela would do everything to see that she was at least happy.

It was the least she could do as a parent. Her own mother hadn't done as much for her. Her mother, rest her soul, had been of the mind that if a child was clothed and fed and had a roof over their head, then everything had been taken care of. But there was so much more to parenting than that. She wished her relationship with her mother had been more... caring.

Thinking back on her time at the house on Glenview Lane, she realized that her entire upbringing had felt like a business transaction. When she had graduated high school and turned eighteen, there was no beating around the bush. Her mother had pushed her from the home like a mama bird kicking a baby out of the nest. She had flown, had found her own way, but she resented her mother for it. She would never do the same thing to Maddie. If Maddie wanted to live at home until she was forty, Angela wouldn't say one word about it.

Angela understood why things had been the way they were between her and her mother... her mother blamed her for her divorce. On the TV shows, when parents divorced, they would have a scene where the child would sob uncontrollably. One of the parents would comfort the child and assure them that it wasn't their fault. Her mother had never done anything of the sort for her. Ann Grimes had never outright blamed her, but there were times when she could feel her mother staring at her and blaming her while she sat at the kitchen table, clipping coupons and chain-smoking Marlboro Lights. She was never without the Marlboro Lights in their gold and white packages.

There were times when she thought it would have been better if her mother had yelled at her, blamed her for breaking up her marriage. As it was, she had grown up walking on eggshells, hiding all of her troubles from her mother for fear of making her hate her even more. Sure, Ann Grimes loved her in her own way. She occasionally even said the words, but it was the kind of love a farmer might have for a dog that got into the chicken coop and killed all the chickens, a tacit, I-made-my-own-bed-now-I'm-going-to-lie-in-it type of love.

Angela had worked to avoid making the mistakes her mother had, and she thought she had done a fine job, up until now. As her mind went over the long-term consequences of the cure, the lamp on the nightstand flickered on and off. It was so quiet in the room, that she could hear the soft clink of the filament going on and off. A cold draft wafted through the cracks of the boarded-up window.

Angela rose from her spot at the end of the bed and walked over to the lamp to see if maybe the bulb wasn't screwed in tight enough. She switched the light off, plunging the room into darkness but for the light from the hallway. Her heart raced as the darkness enveloped her, and she imagined Maddie reaching out towards her in the dark. She reached over the top of the lampshade and hissed as she singed her fingertips on the hot bulb. She pulled her fingers back and instinctively sucked on them. "Damn," she muttered.

"Damn is right," a voice croaked in the dark.

Angela jumped, her hand going to her chest, her heart racing with fear. "Maddie! You scared me," though a part of her knew that it wasn't Maddie she was speaking to. That hadn't been the sweet voice of her daughter... that had been the voice of something else, something... evil. It felt weird to think the word. That word was reserved for movies and alarmist televangelists on the TV.

Maddie just laughed at her, a mocking croak that made her want to run from the room.

"Maddie?" Angela asked, her left hand twisting the light bulb tight in the lamp on the nightstand.

"No," the voice said. "I can feel her in the back of my mind. She wanders in the darkness, wondering where you are. 'Where's Mommy? Where's home?' she calls." The creature on the bed giggled some more.

Angela clenched her jaw and flipped on the light switch. "You're not Maddie," she said to the thing wearing her daughter's body.

The creature smiled, exposing yellowed teeth, broken and sharp. "There is no Maddie. I'm your daughter now. Give me a kiss." The thing on the bed opened those yellowed teeth and shoved out a black and swollen tongue, wiggling the tip in a perverse manner. It laughed on the bed, chuckling maniacally at its own crassness.

Angela put her hand up to her mouth, unwilling to believe what was happening. Tears welled in her eyes, and she wanted to leave, but she stayed, for Maddie.

"I can smell your tears. Let me taste them," the creature called in a sensual voice. "Let me taste your sorrow."

"Shut up," Angela snapped.

"Just drop one onto my tongue. I only need one."

Something in the creature's voice called to her, made her bend down towards the bed, to angle her face toward the creature's open mouth and waggling tongue. Then she straightened up, wondering what had just come over her. "I said shut up," she said, her voice sharp and strong, despite the weakness she felt inside.

That laugh again, that maddening, wicked laugh. It faded, as Angela's hands curled into fists, then the creature crooned, "Oh... your dad says, 'Hello.' He burns in the pits with the others. He says he misses your soft skin."

Angela's hands unclenched, just before her open palm made contact with the creature's face. The skin was hot, moist, the slap echoing off the walls of the room.

More laughter, more mocking chuckles.

Angela snapped and grabbed the creature by the shoulders, shaking her violently. "You shut up! You shut up!" she screamed. She slapped the creature again, forgetting momentarily that this was her daughter's body.

Then Scott was there, pulling her off of the creature. "What are you doing?" he asked, incredulous.

"Help me, Daddy," the creature said in Maddie's voice.

Angela backed away, her hand going to her mouth. "The things she was saying... the things."

"What? What things?" Scott asked.

"Nothing," Angela said, wishing that she had kept her composure, that she hadn't let the creature get to her.

"Mommy has secrets, Daddy," the creature cooed. "But you have your own, don't you?" Those bloodshot eyes focused on Scott, locking in like the scope of a rifle. "Do you remember the boy?"

"I... I don't know what you're talking about," he said. But Angela sensed the lie in his voice. Scott was a terrible liar, but he was great at keeping secrets. He was like an iceberg at times, for the most part, what you saw was what you got, but occasionally, the hull of your boat bumped up against the hidden mass underneath. She didn't like that.

"Oh, I think you do know," the creature said.

"What's she talking about?" Angela asked, though a part of her knew she didn't actually want to know.

"Nothing," Scott said, clipped, short.

"Secret secrets are no fun, secret secrets hurt someone," the creature said in a singsong voice. "Isn't that right, Daddy?" it growled.

Angela saw it happening, saw him losing his composure the way that she had. It began with the clenched jaw, and then would come the clenched fists, then the bunching of the shoulders. His face turned red, and his lips pulsed as held back acidic words.

At this time, Liam entered the room. He took two steps into the room and stopped, his eyes drawn to Maddie, then to Scott standing there and clenching his fists. "What's going on?" he asked.

"Nothing," Scott said, taking a deep breath. "It's just talking, saying nonsense."

Liam nodded his head. "Ignore it. It's just static." Liam moved towards Maddie, and red eyes followed him, locking in on him as they had on Scott.

"You know so much, Mr. Brewster. But you didn't know how to save your own mother, did you? You're not qualified to save anyone, are you?" the creature said.

Angela's ears perked up. There was more truth here. *What did the creature mean "not qualified?"* She was about to ask him what he meant when Liam turned, his face red, from embarrassment or anger, she didn't know. He said, "Come on. Let's go. Everyone out."

He ushered them out, pushing them towards the hallway. Liam looked over his shoulder to see Maddie straining against her bonds, her red eyes following him, her head bobbing from side to side like a cobra ready to strike. There was no smile, only determination on that ugly twisted face. He shivered as he stepped into the hallway, breaking contact with those abyssal eyes.

****

Liam's hands shook as he stalked to the refrigerator, threw open the door, and grabbed a beer. *None of that microbrew shit for the Cutters. Just your standard domestics.* He pulled a Budweiser from the fridge, twisted his wrist and popped the top off. He tossed the bottlecap in the sink with a clink. He tipped the bottle back and took a great swig. The carbonation and coldness burned his throat, but he drank as much as he could handle. When he stopped drinking, half the beer was gone. He smacked his lips and let out a great "Ahhh," not of satisfaction, but of relief. He wiped his mouth with the back of his sleeve, and then noticed Scott and Angela staring at him.

"What was she talking about?" Angela asked him.

He didn't know where to begin. He didn't know how much to tell. He wanted to tell it all. He owed it to them, but then he looked at the big, scarred knuckles on Scott's hands, and he thought better of it. He had experienced the pain knuckles like that could bring when he was a young boy, and then a teenager. "It, Mrs. Cutter. It. It was talking about my mother. She died of cancer a few years ago. There was nothing I could do. I felt so helpless watching her wither away. That's the reason I'm here today..." The words tumbled out of him. He didn't know where they would stop.

****

There wasn't much time left. His mother's life ebbed with each passing second. She lay in the hospital bed, her arms thin and weak, her head bald, her face wasted away until she looked like a propped-up skeleton.

He resisted the urge to cry. He had never been much of a crier. His emotions didn't run deep, as he was frequently too distracted by his own curiosity to examine them. But he had been sitting in the hospital for days now, and the plain, boring hospital room had drained him of all curiosity. He knew what all the machines did. He knew the names of the nurses that did their rounds. He knew the sounds and smells of the hospital. All that was left were his emotions, and his mother as she lay on the bed dying from cancer.

Her eyes fluttered open, and she took a deep, shuddering breath. Her face looked surprised, as if she had never expected to awaken and take another breath again. His body tensed. Was this it? Was this the moment he became an orphan? His father had died some years before of a heart attack, sudden and unexpected. He hadn't loved his father as much as he had loved his mother. His father, Jack, had quite the temper, and there were times when that temper had been turned upon Liam with painful consequences. The sudden loss of his father hadn't hurt, but to see his mother dying was a different story. He felt pain, but it wasn't physical; it was in his chest somewhere, but if someone asked him to point at it, he couldn't have said exactly where it was.

Her eyes remained open, glassy due to the pain medication. They swam around the room, taking in the walls, the unused TV hanging in the air, and then they settled on him. She smiled at him, and he smiled back.

Liam brought his chair closer and wrapped his fingers around her frail hand, squeezing gently. Her fingers were so tiny and delicate. She was only 55 years old, but she seemed much older.

He held a small bottle out to her, a bent straw sticking out of the top. Her lips were dry and cracked. She slept so often now that she wasn't awake enough to keep her lips moistened, and the dry hospital air seemed to suck the moisture right out of her. His mother struggled with the straw, and then she was able to suck weakly on it. He watched the water travel up the clear tube, and then she was coughing. He could swear he could hear her bones grating against each other as she coughed, but that might have been his imagination. He stood and leaned her forward, patting her gently on the back, lest he injure her.

When she finished coughing, she lay back on the pillow, her eyes half-lidded, her breathing heavy and labored.

"You're a good boy," she rasped.

He didn't know what to say. He didn't know what to do. No book he had ever read had prepared him for this.

"You're a good mother," he finally said.

"I'm sorry," she said, shaking her head slightly, tears coming to her eyes.

"You don’t have to be sorry."

""I'm sorry to leave you."

"No, Mom, there's nothing to be sorry for."

She cried a little then, and he did as well.

"I want you to know I'm proud of you."

He let her talk, let her ramble, let herself take her mind wherever she wanted to, and he hung on every word, though later he would forget most of them. She said what she needed to say, though sometimes it didn't make sense. He held her hand and let the tears fall from his face.

She faded quickly, right before his eyes, her words becoming fainter and fainter, and he tried to think of anything that he could do to save her, to make his mom better. But he knew it was hopeless. He wasn't even halfway through medical school yet; he had no real training. All he knew was what he had read and what the doctors had told him.

She looked at him one last time and said, "Let me go."

He didn't understand. He didn't know why she would tell him to let her go.

She gripped his hand hard, and she said it again, "Let me go."

Then her eyes closed. They wouldn't open again. She lay in the bed for another day or two, Liam at her side. Then, she was gone. The doctors and nurses came in and disconnected the equipment, and he sat alone in the room with her. There should have been something he could have done. There had to be a way to save her, even if he didn't know what it was. Despite his mother's words, he couldn't let her go, and he didn't think that he ever would. He carried her like a lump of internal scar tissue wherever he went; everything he did was to help heal that scar and prevent others from having to carry around one of their own. He would never let her go.

****

"Because, even with all of my education, all of my science, there was nothing I could do but watch her disappear. First, her hair. Then her fingernails. Then the spark in her eye..." He could still see her lying on her bed, looking at him with that look, that look that one gets right before they are about to die. "And then she was just gone."

He didn't tell them that she had died alone but for him. He didn't tell them that he was alone, but for the memory of her. It was too much a part of him. It would be like cutting open his chest to expose his own heart. It would be like choosing death.

"I'm sorry," Angela said.

The words did not make him feel better. They couldn't. His emotions had never been strong, and his logical brain knew that someone saying words couldn't make anything feel better. So he did what he always did when someone offered him sympathy. He nodded. "I am too," he said, because he truly was sorry.

From upstairs, the creature in Maddie's bed called in a maniacal, scratchy voice, "Secret secrets! Secret secrets!" She continued yelling the words over and over.

Scott put his hands to his ears. "I don't know how long I can handle this."

It dawned on Angela that there was a way to make the creature stop. It was trying to tear them apart, and it was using their secrets against them. All they had to do was tell their secrets, and then they couldn't be held hostage by the creature upstairs. The hard part would be actually telling her secret. She had held her secrets for years, until they were a part of her, until she didn't even think about them most of the time. They were locked away in a chest in the corner of her mind, and she never visited that corner, never lifted the lid of the chest. But maybe now was the time. The thing upstairs was already so strong, so evil, it only made sense to take away one of its weapons. She said, "Then tell us Scott. Tell us your secret. Once you've let it out, it'll have no power over you."

Scott shook his head and avoided looking at her. "I can't."

"Why?" she asked. She knew why, but he needed to say it.

"It's something I've had to live with forever. I'm afraid of what you'll think."

She saw that he wasn't able to say the words. He wasn't able to take that first step, so she did the only thing she could think of. She told her own story. "Ok, then. I'll go first. Did I ever tell you that my father..." Her voice caught then, and she didn't think that she could continue. Upstairs the creature yelled about secrets again, in that voice, that mocking unnatural voice. "My father used to touch me," she said, squeezing her eyes closed so she wouldn't have to see the looks on their faces, most especially Scott's. "Not anywhere bad," she stammered, "he would just stroke my arm, hold me a little longer than a father should." Her face flushed with blood, the acidic energy of embarrassment coursing through her body. She trailed off then.

"What?" Scott prodded.

Liam took a huge swig of beer, looking as if he wanted to be anywhere else but in the Cutter's kitchen at that moment.

"He never did anything." She wanted them to be clear on that. "But I could tell that he wanted to. Mom could tell too. That's why she divorced him. We never really spoke about it; we didn't really have to. Sometimes, after the divorce, when I would walk home from high school, I would see him parked down a side street watching me. I told my mom about it, and she said to just ignore him. I hated her for that. He was my father; he was a person, but she wanted nothing to do with him. As time went on, I began to imagine that my mother had made it all up. When I saw him, I wanted to wave, to acknowledge that he was there, but I was too afraid of what Mother would say. Then, when I was ten, I stopped seeing him altogether."

Scott reached out with a comforting hand as she lapsed into silence. Angela shrugged him off. She didn't want his comfort. This was her secret, one that she had held so long that she didn't really need comfort, she just needed the courage to tell it.

"He died alone, with no one there. The neighbors smelled his body, and they contacted us because we were his only next of kin. He hung himself. All he left was a picture of me. On the back he wrote, 'I never meant to hurt you,' and to this day, I wonder... was I wrong? Were we both wrong?"

Liam finished the beer at the kitchen counter. He said nothing, but he wore his discomfort like a cloak. He set the glass bottle down and moved to the fridge for another beer.

"You can't blame yourself," Scott said.

Angela glared at Scott, steel in her eyes. "I don't." She meant it too. There was nothing that she had ever done or could have done to fix the broken parts of her childhood. She had been a child. The adults were supposed to be looking out for her, watching over her. "I never told anyone because I just didn't want people to know. It's my business, my personal business, and it's all in the past. None of it matters anymore. But of course it does, or else I would have talked about it a long time ago." She sighed, embarrassment swimming in her blood, but somehow she felt unburdened as well.

Liam handed her a beer, and she put the cool bottle to her head and closed her eyes feeling revulsion at what everyone must think of her. But that was not why she was here. Her issues were not why they were sharing secrets. They had work to do. They had a little girl to save upstairs, and when this was all over, her daughter would have secrets of her own to carry with her for the rest of her life, but at least she would have a "rest of her life." She popped the top off of the beer and then turned to Scott. "Now you go." She put no comfort into the words. She had bared her biggest secret, had done a damn concise job of it too. Now there was no excuse that he could make for not sharing.

"I can't," he said. Angela resisted the urge to punch him. Instead, she said, "If I can tell, you can tell. You have to. No secrets. We have to be strong. Tell me."

Seemingly out of thin air, Liam thrust a beer before Scott's face. He looked at it thoughtfully, and then waved it off. He looked down at the floor, massaging an invisible spot on one of his hands, and then began his tale, unable to make eye contact. "When I was in high school, I went to a party. There was beer. Maybe I drank too much."

He looked up at her, and then shook his head, dropping his eyes to the floor once again. "No. That's not true. I know I drank too much. I shouldn't have been out there. I shouldn't have been behind the wheel." He slumped down at the kitchen table, rubbing at an imagined piece of dirt on his hands.

"He came out of nowhere. He was a boy, my age. I heard about it at school the next day. Someone had run over Timmy Lipscomb."

****

Scott stumbled from the party. That should have been his first sign that he shouldn't have been driving. He hadn't intended to drink so much, but as the only brown person at an all-white party, he had felt like he had to prove himself, especially when Will King had started calling him a pussy in front of the girls.

He saw Rachel Pierce looking at him, measuring him, and his machismo stepped to the forefront. He saw Jenny Tucker, the girl he had been crushing on since middle school, arch an eyebrow, and there he had been, the end of a dirty beer bong in his mouth, choking down Natty

Ice as gravity pushed it down his throat and into his stomach. One beer, two, three… and then he had lost count.

Now he was drunk, and for what? He had seen Rachel disappear into a backroom with Austin Marks, the biggest dirtbag in school. He was the type of guy that would let you know how many fingers he had slipped into his latest conquest. Jenny Tucker, always so pure and wholesome, had disappeared about an hour after his first drink, and he knew he had missed his opportunity to say something to her, anything. Instead he had been stuck at Will King's country house, drinking beer, which he loathed.

Scott was under no illusions. He was a second-class citizen in many of the other students' eyes, but he didn't want to be. He wanted to fit in. He wanted them to see him as just one of the guys, as a friend without the qualifier of his race, so he had stayed and tried to impress them with his ability to hold his alcohol.

Despite the moving keyhole on his car door, he managed to unlock the door. He swung the door open and plopped inside his Ford Escort. It wasn't a great car, nothing special, but it was a car, and it afforded him the status that he needed to avoid being one of the poor kids in the eyes of the other students at school, though he was still technically a poor kid. He didn't think Jenny Tucker would be interested in someone without money, so he had slaved in his father's garage, doing oil changes, learning how to install brake pads, and generally tidying up the place. Scott had cobbled together enough money to buy the car, and just like that, he had started getting invited to the parties in the sticks.

Now all he needed was a girlfriend. But that would have to wait for another night. He had considered spending the night at Will's, but Howard Kelly had started throwing veiled racist stereotypes in his direction, and he didn't think that the evening was going to get anymore civil as it wore on. As it was, he had to resist the urge to beat the shit out of

Howard. He really deserved it though. He was a no-good piece of shit and always had been.

He turned the key and threw the car into drive. Scott accidentally drove over part of the lawn in the attempt to turn around. He was sure he would hear about that at school. It was a nice lawn. People like Will's parents loved their lawns.

He went slow down the country lane, shaking his head and squinting his eyes as he tried to keep the car on the gravel road. He contemplated pulling over to the side, but he knew his dad would question him about it if he showed up at home any later than he was already going to be. He really had no choice. Stay at Will's and risk getting into a fight with Howard or some other ignorant idiot or leave when he was sober and face the wrath of his old man for staying out so late? The fact that the way home was mostly comprised of backroads made up his mind for him. He would drive.

The night was dark, and there was no one else on the country lanes. He turned his music up as loud as it would go, the shitty speakers rattling. But he didn't care. He didn't have a care in the world. He turned on his brights, chasing away the darkness of the gloomy road and hoping that he didn't hit a deer on his way back into town. His dad would kill him if he damaged the car, and they had to file an insurance claim. There were a lot of things his dad would kill him for, but he was still alive, so he must be doing something right.

He made it off the gravel road and onto Route 12, and from there, he expected smooth sailing. He floored the accelerator, enjoying the pickup of the Escort. It was a cheap car, but it went fast when he wanted it to, and something about the buzz in his head and the music on the radio, the rattling of the speakers, made him want to go fast.

"Few times I been around that track, so it's not just gonna happen like that, cause I ain't no hollaback girl, I ain't no hollaback girl!"

He was belting Gwen Stefani's latest jam, when another car careened around the corner out of the darkness. Its headlights splashed across his eyes temporarily blinding him. Instinctively, he swerved to the side to avoid hitting the car, and over the blare of his stereo, he heard the car honk its horn as its taillights disappeared into the night. He stomped on the brakes to avoid winding up in a ditch, the right wheels of his car on the dirt shoulder, and the left wheels on the pavement. The differential between the two surfaces forced his car to shoot across the road, his car spinning out of control as he screamed. He came to a stop in a ditch, facing the opposite direction he had been headed.

"Oh, fuck, oh fuck." He did a quick check. The engine still gurgled. He didn't feel injured. There were no cops around. As quick as he could, he spun the car around and got headed back in the right direction.

He turned off his brights, and he decided to drive home at the speed limit. He turned the radio off, and he was doing everything by the book, minus a little swerving and being obviously drunk behind the wheel. All that was left for him, was one last hairpin turn, and then he would be off the country road, and back into the main part of town. Home free, he thought. He misjudged the turn, his car outpacing the pool of light his car provided as he careened around the bend. There was a thump as his car made contact with something. He saw a flash of color, the shine of headlights on metal. His heart racing in his chest, he drove on for a hundred yards, and then he stopped the car safely on the side of the road.

He tried to pretend that nothing was wrong. He tried to pretend that he hadn't done anything wrong at all, that he could still go home, and everything would be fine. But his body knew differently. His heart thumped in his chest, and his mouth was so dry that his tongue felt like it was sticking to the roof of his mouth. *Well, there's no use sitting around until a cop comes along or something.*

He threw open the door of the car and ran back to see what he had hit. Scott expected to hear some sort of crying, thrashing, or moaning from an animal… or even a person. But there was nothing, just the sound of his own blood pumping in his ears. He pulled his cell phone out, and flipped it open. It was more of a flashlight than anything else. His dad didn't let him text or make phone calls on it. He always said, "We ain't made of money," whenever the bill came in, and Scott had inevitably texted a couple of his wealthier friends. His dad worried about him whenever he went out. Their town wasn't small, but many of the people in it were. The phone offered his dad some peace of mind.

By the faint glow of his flip phone, Scott spotted the metallic gleam of a twisted bike frame. His stomach dropped, and he thought he was going to throw up. A bike… oh shit.

He panned the light around the woods and caught a hint of a reflective vest lying in a patch of grass under a tree. He saw the body. His life flashed before his eyes. He was going to go to jail. He was going to be the guy that killed someone while drunk driving. He had no future. His whole life was over. He stepped closer to the body, to take a closer look. By moving his phone around he was able to make out the twisted form of… Timmy Lipscomb. He knew the owner of that skinny, boyish face. It belonged to Timmy Lipscomb, the kid that sat next to him in math class doodling wizards in his notebook rather than paying attention to the teacher.

Scott backed away. He wanted to help; he wanted to do anything but what he was actually doing. He looked down at his phone and contemplated dialing 911. But in the end, his own life came first, and with a heart full of guilt, he ran back to his car, tears in his eyes.

He drove away from Timmy Lipscomb, speeding his way back home, needing to get as far away as he could. At home, he parked the car in the garage, his heart hammering in his chest. The right front fender of his car was dented heavily, the headlight smashed. He sat in the garage for half an hour wondering what he should do. Then he took a deep shuddering breath, and he walked upstairs and went to bed, calling himself a coward and an idiot all night long. For weeks afterwards, he would dream of that night, of swerving around a corner and making full contact with Timmy Lipscomb. Only, in his dreams, Timmy splattered against the windshield, asking, "Why?" over and over.

****

Angela's hand went to her mouth.

"Did you kill him?" Liam asked, his face flushed from the beer.

Scott shook his head. "No. He survived. But he never walked again. I never told anyone. My parents never asked about the car, but I knew they knew. My dad patched up the fender. I walked to school for months. But the worst part was knowing that I missed my opportunity to make it right. Maybe if I had called the police, they could have taken him to the hospital. Maybe they could have helped him."

Scott looked down at his hands, rubbing them awkwardly. Angela put her hand on his shoulder and said nothing. She gave him quiet support, not forgiveness, not acceptance.

Scott looked up at the ceiling and squeezed his eyes shut. "How does that thing in there know things that we've never told anyone?"

"Father Romero would say it's a tool of the devil and that the devil knows our weaknesses," Liam said.

Angela turned to Liam, her arm still resting on Scott's shoulder. "You don't even believe in God, let alone the devil."

Liam sighed then. "It's hard to look that thing upstairs in the eye and pretend it's not comprised of pure evil, especially when it can see inside you... inside your heart."

"I don't even want to go back in there," Angela said, surprised at her words.

"But we have to. We can't leave it unguarded. If it escaped, who knows what would happen?"

Scott spoke then, lifting himself from his own self-loathing long enough to ask a question. "How long until I get my daughter back?"

Liam said, "I'll keep running the tests. As soon as we have proof that the cancer is gone, we'll get that thing, whatever it is, out of her."

A thought dawned on Angela, and she spoke the words aloud. "What if she doesn't get better? What if nothing changes?"

Liam looked at Angela then, adjusting his glasses. "Then I will be apologizing to you two for the rest of my life.

****

Angela sat in a chair in Maddie's room. The chair was no longer at the foot of the bed. She couldn't bring herself to sit that close to the creature in Maddie's skin. She felt its presence, like a clammy summer fog. She smelled its presence as well, a foul stench, faint enough that she could trick herself into thinking that the smell was all in her imagination, but it was there. She knew that.

Her hands and mind kept busy with knitting, the clicking of the needles soothing her soul. On the bed, Maddie stirred, breathing heavily, her head twisting from side to side. She appeared to be in the midst of a nightmare.

Then Angela noticed something. On top of Maddie's head there was a darkening. She placed her knitting needles down on the chair and walked over to Maddie. She placed a hand on her head and ran her palm across Maddie's scalp. *Stubble.* Her hair was growing back. She smiled then. *It was going to work. It was working.* If her hair was growing back, then maybe other things were getting back to normal as well. Maybe the cancer was gone already.

Maddie's eyes snapped open, red, blood-filled eyes, two black pupils swimming in the blood. Maddie's lips pulled back exposing a toothy smile of jagged, rotting teeth. Her eyes flashed with a terrible light, so dark, so... penetrating. Angela rocked backwards as the light washed over her. She felt a tingling energy flowing through her body.

"Untie me," Maddie whispered.

Of course, Angela thought. It made no sense to have her daughter tied up. She was all better now. Anyone could see that. Her hands moved slowly around Maddie's left foot, stumbling to find the trick of the knot. The knot came free finally, and then she stood there, trying to remember what she was supposed to be doing. *Knitting?*

"Good, now the other one," Maddie said.

Yes, of course... Maddie needed to be untied. She moved slowly to the other side of the bed. It was hard moving. It was harder still even to think. She began fiddling with the knot of the jump rope. The thick plastic beads encasing the rope made it hard.

Scott walked into the room. *Oh, good, someone to help untie Maddie. Maybe he would have more luck untying this knot.*

"Angela?" he asked, confusion on his face.

She continued working at the knot. She could only do one thing at a time it seemed. Either she could untie the knot, or she could talk to Scott. Untying the knot seemed to be the most important thing to do.

"Angela? What are you doing?" Scott asked.

Ah, success. The knot of the jump rope finally came undone, and she pulled it free. Now, all she had to do was free Maddie's arms. She probed the rope binding Maddie's right hand, looking for a way into the knot, a way to loosen it and eventually break it free. Then Maddie could help her with the other knot. Her little fingers would probably be better at it.

"Don't do that," Scott said.

Don't do what? She was just trying to free Maddie.

Scott, panic filling him, dove across Maddie and slapped away Angela's hands from the rope binding Maddie's hand to the bed. He didn't know what had come over Angela, but he knew that if she managed to free Maddie, something bad was very likely to happen. She continued to make progress as Scott tried to keep her hands away from the knot. "Liam! I need some help in here!" he called.

Maddie laughed as the knot loosened a bit. She began wriggling her wrist, struggling to get loose from the rope, aching to be free.

"Liam!" Scott called again, his voice bellowing through the house. Liam skidded into the room. His eyes took in the situation from behind his glasses, but he seemed frozen. "Stop her!" Scott yelled.

Liam rushed to Angela and pulled her away from the bed. Her hands stayed out in front of her like a movie monster from the fifties, still pawing at the air, as if she were still untying the knot.

Maddie managed to slip her hand free from the loosened rope, and immediately she grasped a handful of

Scott's hair, wrenching his head to the side. She pulled so hard that he was thrown from the bed, landing on the floor with a thump.

Liam dove and took his place, fighting to hold onto Maddie's free arm as she struggled to reach across her body to undo the other knot. Maddie scratched and clawed at Liam, drawing blood in several places.

As Scott got to his feet to help Liam, he noticed Angela still standing, trying to untie knots in the air. Scott dove on top of Liam and Maddie. She was frightfully strong, almost stronger than he and Liam combined, but not quite.

"Angela! Wake up!" he called. They couldn't hold Maddie down and tie her up as well.

Maddie lunged forward with her mouth, clamping down on Liam's neck with her jagged teeth. He thrashed on the bed, screaming in pain, blood running down his face from several scratches. "Get her off me!" he shrieked.

Scott reached over Liam and slipped a finger between Maddie's teeth and her cheek, fish-hooking her. She turned, her mouth opening to release Liam's neck, and snapped at his finger. He barely pulled it back in time, or he surely would have lost a finger.

"Angela! Snap out of it!" he called.

The bed began to quake, tossing Liam and Scott about. The lights in the room flickered, and from the corner of his eye, he saw Angela shake her head as if trying to clear the cobwebs. She looked at her hands, still hanging in midair, fingers wriggling as if still trying to untie knots. She stared at her hands wonderingly.

"Angela!" Liam called.

"Help us!" Scott called.

Angela jumped into action, still trying to piece together everything that had just happened. She grabbed Maddie's free arm, recoiling slightly from the cold, damp flesh. She pulled her near the post, using every ounce of strength that she possessed. She wrapped the rope around Maddie's wrist, and worked as fast as she could, her fingers feeling clumsy and awkward. "I got it!" she said, backing away from the bed and Maddie's scowling face.

Scott and Liam climbed off of Maddie, thankful that the ordeal was over. They moved around the bed to tie down Maddie's feet. She kicked and kicked at them, sending Liam flying once, but in the end, they were able to tie that leg down as well. When they had finally secured Maddie, Liam stood back, rubbing the spot on his chest where Maddie had kicked him and grimacing in pain.

The creature on the bed thrashed violently, grunting in frustration. The bonds held tight. As if a switch were flipped, the creature stopped struggling. It regarded each of them with an icy stare. Angela could see the fury behind those eyes. The creature opened its mouth and let loose a demonic howl. The walls shook with the force of it. Plaster sifted down from the ceiling.

Scott put his hands to his ears to block the sound. He saw Liam and Angela do the same.

Then, as suddenly as a summer rain shower, it was over, and the creature glared at them once again. "I almost had you," it said in a quiet voice.

The adults removed their hands from their ears but said nothing. "I would have had you all. We'd all freeze together."

"Shut up," Liam said in disgust.

"We'd freeze like Momma," it said.

"Shut up."

"Do you know what she does in hell, Mr. Brewster?" the creature asked, laughing. "She lays on a bed. Her hair comes out in clumps. Her fingernails turn black and fall off. She vomits until her intestines come out of her mouth. And then you show up. She asks you to help her, and you do nothing. You just sit there, just like you did in real life."

Liam's fists balled up and Scott could see he was close to the breaking point. It was reassuring to actually see an emotional response from him. The boy looked like a nightmare with a burn mark on his cheeks, a bite mark on his neck, and scratches all over his face. Scott put a restraining hand on Liam's shoulder and said, "That's what it wants. Don't give it the satisfaction."

The creature continued, twisting the knife. "Then Momma dies, and it starts all over again." It threw back its head and cackled.

Liam took a deep breath, and then he smiled. "Even if there were a hell, I know you're lying because my mother wouldn't be there."

The creature contorted Maddie's face into a mocking frown. "You're no fun. I'm just trying to have some fun."

Scott had seen enough. He pulled Liam by the shoulder and prodded him toward the exit. Once he got Liam out of the room, he waved Angela over. "Come on, Angela," he said. Angela walked over, ignoring the lewd gestures from the being on the bed.

Once in the hallway, Liam bent over and grabbed his knees, a burst of breath escaping his lungs. Scott leaned back against the wall, wincing briefly as his bruised head bumped against the drywall. The back of his head was still tender from the damage it had sustained over the last couple of days. He ran his hand through his hair, finding it surprisingly sweaty. Angela stood in the hallway, looking somewhat dazed and confused. "What the hell happened in there?" she asked in a fog.

Scott said, "She's getting stronger. She tossed me to the side like a ragdoll. Somehow she hypnotized you... or... or something." He realized the words sounded stupid, unbelievable. But there was no getting around it. It was what it was. "And then she had you untie her. If she had gotten free, I don't know that we could have stopped her."

He took a deep breath and then turned to Liam. "I think we need to end this now. Liam, is she going to get any stronger than this?"

"God, I hope not," he said.

Scott resisted the urge to sock the kid. Angela just stared at him in disbelief. "You hope not? You don't know?"

"Yeah, how bad is this going to get, Liam?"

Liam adjusted his glasses, a mannerism that Scott had come to despise. "I'm not sure."

Scott advanced on Liam, fighting his desire to pummel that smug, baby face. He should have asked these questions to begin with, before they had ever agreed to go through with his cure, but he hadn't because of that spark of hope in his chest. He hadn't wanted to dampen it, extinguish it, because then, it could only mean death for Maddie. But now, his daughter was in even more risk. *Her soul,* Father Romero had said. "How many of these things have you studied?"

"As many as I could," he said somewhat evasively.

"Give us a number!" Scott shouted.

"I could only find solid evidence of the one case—"

Angela interrupted him, "One? One freaking case? You had us do this to our daughter on the basis of one case."

Liam seemed to grasp their fury. "I understand you're mad."

"Mad doesn't even begin to cover it, pal," Scott said.

Liam looked at them, impassionate. "But it's working. You have to see that."

"It's a nightmare," Angela said.

"But it's going to work. I know it."

"Well how bad did that girl get? What was her name?" Scott grasped in his memory for the name. "Katie! That's it. How bad did it get with her?"

Liam adjusted his glasses again, and Scott resisted the urge to snatch them off his face and snap them in half. "I looked into it, but no one wanted to talk about it. I did stumble across some medical files of a couple of her immediate family members. Her parents suffered a few broken bones, an orbital fracture, some serious abrasions and scratches."

"Oh, is that all?" Angela asked mockingly. She laughed and turned to Scott. "A few broken bones, some scratches."

"You didn't let me finish. There was also one death. It turns out the priest in the video wasn't the first to try and perform an exorcism on Katie."

Scott was in a state of shock. Why hadn't he asked these questions before everything had started? How stupid could he be? "Why didn't you tell us any of this?" He laughed at his own adroitness. "Wait. I already know the answer. Because then we wouldn't have gone through with this stupid idea in the first place."

From the first floor, they heard a deep, sonorous voice call up to them. "He also would have had to explain that he isn't even a doctor yet. He's a first-year medical student who happened to be working at the hospital when Katie was admitted." It was Father Romero. He climbed the stairs, appearing to rise out of thin air, his face drawn and serious. In his hands he held a leather messenger bag with a gold cross emblazoned upon the side.

"What are you talking about?" Angela asked.

Scott knew what he was talking about. He supposed he had always known it, but he had been too scared to make a point of it.

"Liam is no scientist... no doctor," Father Romero fairly spit. "He hasn't even graduated yet."

Liam stood in the hallway, denying nothing. The only sign that he even heard Father Romero was a blushing in his cheeks and a self-conscious readjustment of his glasses. He rocked on his heels, and then he said, "It's true."

Scott rushed at Liam then. He grabbed the front of his shirt in his fists, and then he lifted up Liam and slammed him against the wall. "I ought to end you right now." He was about to cock back his arm, when he felt a hand on his shoulder. He turned, expecting to see Angela. She abhorred violence. Instead, he saw the serious face of Father Romero looking him dead in the eye. "But you're not going to end him, Scott."

"Oh yeah? And why not?"

"Because it's God's job to decide when it's Liam's time. And if you had listened to God in the first place, we wouldn't be in this mess to begin with."

Scott let Liam slide to the ground. "You're right. You always were. This isn't Liam's fault. It's mine... because I couldn't let go." Scott knew the truth in those words.

"Neither could I," Angela said.

"None of that is important now. The past is immutable. Right now, we have a sick girl in there, and she needs our help. We have to get the demon out now." His words carried a sense of urgency that raised Scott's concern.

"But what about her cancer?" Liam asked.

"What good is a healthy body without a soul, Mr. Brewster?"

Father Romero's words struck Liam into silence. He merely nodded.

"Now we have a lot of work to do. It's going to be a long night."

Scott asked, "What are you going to do, Father?"

"Well, first, I'm going to need a pot of coffee. After that, I'm going to send that demon straight to Hell."

Chapter 10: Exorcism

Father Romero stood in Maddie's bedroom dressed in his finest robe. A green stole was draped over his shoulders. He knelt on the floor, feeling the burden of age in his knees. He felt the stare of the creature on the bed, but he refused to acknowledge it. He ran his hand across the cover of the leather-bound book in front of him. The book was ancient, unnamed, and within it, there were rituals that all priests hoped they would never have to invoke.

The creature growled at him. He could sense its fear, its trepidation. But Father Romero paid it no mind. God was on his side. He opened the book, leafing through the thin, onion-skin pages until he found the section that he was looking for. It had been years since he had read the book, years since he had studied it under the guidance of his mentor. Once his lessons had been over, he had buried it in a back room of the church, for he did not like to be reminded of the fact that there were beings like the creature that inhabited Maddie. He found the passage he was looking for and read it and re-read it.

Then he closed the cover of the book and stood up. He closed his eyes and envisioned the words, etching them in his mind's eye. He raised his head to the sky and muttered the words, trying them on for size. He placed the book on the bed, between Maddie's bound ankles. Maddie hissed and struggled on the bed, trying to move as far away from the book as her bindings would let her.

Father Romero drained the dregs of a cup of coffee. He thought it might be a Costa Rican blend, but he couldn't be sure. He stood up and pronounced, "I'm ready!"

The door flung open, and Angela and Scott strode into the room, crosses painted on their faces with the gray ash of a few burned pages from the Bible. Their faces were emotionless, empty. *Good, that is as it should be. Emotions could be turned, perverted. They mustn't offer the creature any sort of advantage.*

Liam entered after, a camera perched on his shoulders. Father Romero had tried to talk the boy out of it, but he would not be swayed. Since the boy was unneeded for the ritual, he had assented, mostly as a matter of expediency. Let him play his games; he was trying to save Maddie and had no time to argue. It didn't matter if it was recorded or not. Still, he decided to give it one more shot. "Get that thing out of here."

Liam shook his head and said, "The world has to see."

It was as he thought. The boy would not change his mind. "If you're not going to take it out of here, then stay out of the way."

Maddie smiled at the camera, or rather, the creature did. He had to stop thinking of the thing on the bed as Maddie, or else the ritual would be that much harder. "I'm going to be a star," it said, smiling into the camera.

Father Romero directed Scott and Angela to their spots. He had gone through the ritual with them. They were as important as he was. "Over here, Scott. Angela, I need you on this side." They stood near the foot of the bed and placed their hands upon Maddie's bare feet.

"Just like that. Your bodies are buffers. Your blood is her blood. Your blood is the blood of Christ. It flows in you. It will buffer you and bind you to Maddie and to her soul." He pulled the blade from his vestments, an ornate silver knife handed down from priest to priest, consecrated, forged in the bowels of the Vatican by priestsmiths. He ran the blade down Angela's arm. She winced in pain as her skin parted and the blood started to flow down her skin and onto Maddie's foot. The creature screamed in pain as the blood touched it. He repeated the process with Scott.

"Whatever you do, do not let go. The blood binds her and dampens the demon's powers," he instructed.

"Yes, Father," Angela said. Scott merely nodded.

Father Romero watched as Liam swooped around the far side of the bed, his camera taking in everything. Maddie howled in pain, thrashing her head from side to side. The light in the bedroom began to flicker. A small wind kicked up, the stench of death carried upon it. The window curtains rippled like underwater weeds on the edge of a swollen riverbank.

Father Romero locked eyes with the creature. Maddie was in there somewhere, and he was going to bring her out. "I don't suppose you want to make this easy for me and just tell me your name."

"I have no name," it snarled.

"Well then," he said. It was as he expected it to be. Never, in all his studies had he ever heard of a demon giving its name freely. He was going to have to work for it. He touched the rosary he had used to mark the appropriate passage in the book, and he flipped it open. "We'll just do it the hard way." He produced an aspergillum from his pocket, a brass ball at the end, perforated with holes to allow holy water to sprinkle through. He raised his arm and brought the aspergillum down, splattering the creature with holy water. It landed on her skin with a hiss, and steam rose from her body. From the corners of his eyes, he saw Angela and Scott flinch. He hoped they could be strong. He hoped they would be able to see this through.

"In the name of Jesus, our Lord, I rebuke thee." He splashed the creature again, producing another hiss and more steam. "Father, I your terrestrial servant, beseech you to lend me the strength and the will to banish this atrocity from the paradise you made for us."

"Fuck you!" the creature screamed before Father Romero splashed it again. This time, the creature's skin split wide open, like a hot dog left on the grill too long, exposing the red flesh inside. Angela gasped, but Father Romero had no time to comfort her. The flesh began to knit together immediately. The creature kicked and thrashed wildly, and Angela lost her grip.

"Hold her! Don't lose contact!" Father Romero implored. Angela gripped Maddie's foot tighter.

Father Romero continued the ritual. "This creature, this mockery, is an affront to all that you have made. Lend me your power, Lord, so that I might smite this fiend and send it from whence it came." Father Romero raised his hand high in the air, as the unholy stench of the dead washed over him. His eyes filled with a golden light and the creature locked eyes with him.

"Go away!" she screamed, fear edging into its voice for the first time.

Father Romero's skin felt like it was stretching across his entire body, so tight, he thought he was going to explode. He focused his mind, turning it into a knife, every bit as sharp as the one he had used to slice open Scott and Angela's arms. He focused his mind on his fist, and he felt the power, felt the glory of his God concentrate in his fist until he was sure it was about to explode in a shower of bones, tendons, and blood.

"You don't belong here!" the creature cried, though it was not talking to Father Romero. "You have forsaken us!"

Father Romero was deaf to the creature's blasphemy. Its words were subterfuge, smoke and mirrors meant to distract. He brought the aspergillum to his lips and gave it a kiss. He felt the power suffusing his body enter into the water contained within. When he held it in the air, the aspergillum glowed golden and pure. He brought his arm down, sprinkling the creature. The demon howled in pain, and the room quaked with its rage. The wounds the holy water made were larger this time, frightfully larger. Where it had contacted Maddie's leg, he could see the bone. The flesh began to knit back together, but not nearly as fast as before.

"You're killing her!" Scott shouted.

"She's already dead! We're going to bring her back!" Father Romero countered, as the room filled with a rushing wind. The curtains over the boarded-up window swirled, as dust and leaves entered the room through the cracks between the wooden boards. The entire time, the creature on the bed screamed, nonsensical guttural sounds.

Suddenly, the lamp on the nightstand burst, showering them with broken glass and sparks. The room plunged into darkness, and Father Romero fought down an overwhelming wave of fear.

"I can't see!" Scott yelled over the howling of Maddie and the rushing wind.

Father Romero yelled, "Don't lose touch! It's getting stronger!"

"Liam, does that camera have a light?" Angela called.

"I'm trying," Liam said.

"Hurry up, man," Father Romero said, panic welling in his brain as his mind filled in the darkness with all sorts of horrors.

"I think I found it," Liam shouted. Shortly after, the camera's light finally came on. It was an inadequate light, only illuminating a small part of the room at any one time.

Father Romero watched that small circle of light as it focused on Scott and Angela breathing heavy, their blood-covered hands holding Maddie's feet. The pool of light slid across her legs where there was no evidence of the wounds created by the holy water. The light slid across her torso, showing blood-soaked clothing. Then the light hit Maddie's face, monstrous, distorted. It was the type of face one might see in a carnival mirror, distorted, shifting, as if it didn't know what it wanted to be. The creature emitted a low, guttural laugh, and then brought its hands into the weak light from Liam's camera.

"She's loose," Father Romero said, his voice a wheezing whisper of fear.

"How would you know, Father? Have you been a naughty boy?"

"Get her!" Scott yelled at Liam.

Liam set his camera down on the bed, the light barely illuminating the shadows. Father Romero rushed around the bed to join him in tying her back up. She slashed at them with razor-clawed fingertips and pummeled them with stone-like fists as they fought to grip her arms. The smack of her fist against his own flesh rang in the priest's ears.

Together, they were able to grab one of her arms and inch it towards the metal railing of the bed. It moved closer and closer, and then, with a sudden burst of strength, she broke her arm loose. There was a brief moment of pain, and then Father Romero was lying on the floor clutching at his face. He reached up to touch the wounds and screamed in pain as his brain finally registered what had happened. He could not see. His eyes... they were gone.

Father Romero didn't know what to do. He didn't know how to understand the world around him without eyes. The priest moaned on the floor, not even sure which way was up. The pain threatened to overtake him, and his first instinct was to get to his feet and run from the room, but he refused his fears. He had known the risks. He would see this through. He had made a promise.

He could hear the creature howling with laughter on the bed. "An eye for an eye... isn't that what the Bible says, Father?"

****

Liam finished tying up Maddie's right hand, and he set about securing her left, just as he saw her stab a finger into her own eye. He winced in pain and wondered just how far the demon's regenerative properties would go. Surely, they couldn't replace an eye. As he wrestled with Maddie, these thoughts ran through his head, but little else. He was aware of Scott and Angela screaming at the top of their lungs, the foul wind rushing through the room, and the pitiable moans of Father Romero on the floor. He didn't know what had happened to the priest, but the fact that he was still making noise was as good a sign as any.

Scott and Angela screamed at him, unintelligible words. He was too busy trying to secure Maddie to the bed to focus on what they were yelling.

Finally, he managed to secure her second arm, and he climbed off of the icy form on the bed. The coldness of Maddie's skin... she felt like a dead body. He had encountered a few at the hospital, but never that cold.

He grabbed his camera from the bed and trained it on Maddie. She smiled at him, covered in slimy sweat that he was all too familiar with from wrestling with her arms. Her remaining eye, glowed with a cold blue light, but he was glad to see that the other one was slowly knitting itself back together.

The room quaked then, knocking him slightly off balance, the light of the camera swinging around the room. Maddie began to babble, harsh, dark words that seemed to hang in the air and echo before she was even done speaking them. Upon hearing another of Father Romero's moans, he aimed the camera at his feet. Father Romero rolled on the floor clutching at his face. Liam squatted down with the camera to pull Father Romero's hands away from his eyes.

"Is he ok?" Angela asked from the darkness behind him.

"Are you ok, Father?" Liam asked.

Father Romero removed his hands and looked up at him. Liam winced in sympathetic pain. Those steel blue eyes had been replaced by rough, red wounds, deep enough that the light from the camera didn't penetrate them.

Streams of blood ran down his cheeks, and Liam turned away from the red pits of his eye sockets.

"I can't see. I'm blind," Father Romero called, his hands waving in front of him, searching for anything to grab hold of. "I do not have an exact memory of the exorcism rites," he said.

Liam didn't know how Father Romero could sound so calm. "How are we going to finish this?" Liam asked, his heart starting to beat faster. The creature on the bed gnashed its teeth at him, as another howl of foul wind swept through the room.

"No!" Scott wailed. "You have to finish it, Father!"

"You'll have to do it, Liam," Father Romero said.

The words had a weight to them, and they threatened to force him down to the ground. "What?" Liam asked, still unsure if he had heard the priest correctly.

"The passages are marked," Father Romero said from the floor. "You'll have to read them."

"I can't," Liam said.

But Father Romero forged on, among the howls from Maddie, the wind, the heavy breathing from all of them, "Angela and Scott must bind Maddie to this earth with their still-warm blood. I can't see. That only leaves you."

Liam's head swam. He had always planned to go through with the ritual, to repeat what the priest in the video had done, but Father Romero's ritual was different. And on top of that, he had one little issue that seemed to be lacking... faith. He had seen the golden light filling Father Romero's body. He had sensed the presence of something, but deep down, he still didn't believe. "I can't perform an exorcism," he stated flatly.

Maddie thrashed on the bed, spitting in the direction of Father Romero, but he ignored her, most likely because he couldn't see what she was doing. "You're not performing anything. God is. Let go, and let God do his work."

Liam shook his head as Scott and Angela implored him to try. He set the camera down on the ground, light shining up at his face. He bent down and picked up the strange book that Father Romero had been reading from. He would give anything to be able to study the book. He almost recoiled at the feel of the book's cover. It was cold, skin-like. He looked at the pages, doubt on his face.

"You can do it!" Angela said, the howling wind in the room swirling her hair about her head.

"Ok... uhh... let me see," he began tentatively. He felt like a fool, but he said the words anyway, "This vessel is a holy vessel, one of divine design. You are not welcome inside of it." On the page, written in red ink, he saw instructions. He lifted up the aspergillum and flicked his arm, splashing Maddie with water. Nothing happened. The wind in the room blew stronger, and Liam was forced to hold the pages of the book down awkwardly with the aspergillum still held in his hand.

Maddie laughed in response. "You don't have what it takes, college boy." Maddie's eyes, the destroyed one fully regenerated now, filled with a blue light, a light like the shadowy underside of a snow bank. The light hurt to look at, but at least he could read the words in the book better, though, based upon how it was going so far, that didn't seem to matter.

"The Lord defies your presence," he yelled, feeling embarrassed and foolish at the same time. "Go back from whence you came." He flung the holy water, and again nothing happened.

"How long are you going to keep this up? It becomes tiresome," Maddie said, straining at her bonds. Liam felt panic rise as he saw the metal bar her hand was bound to begin to bend.

"The Lord defies your presence. Go back from whence you came!" he shouted, using the panic to make his voice more powerful, more commanding.

"You have to believe, Liam. You have to believe," Father Romero implored from the floor.

"But I don't believe," he spat back, his voice accompanied by laughter from Maddie.

In a forlorn voice, Father Romero said, "Then she is truly lost."

"Come on, man," Scott begged. "For Maddie, please, just believe. You gotta believe," Scott said, tears and fear in his eyes.

"You can do it, Liam," Angela said, her voice motherly and surprisingly soothing among the chaos of Maddie's room. "He's real. Believe in Him."

On the bed, Maddie's skin began to show fine cracks, the skin darkening as it came apart. That cold, snowbank light shone through the cracks. Maddie threw back her head and emitted a deep bellow, like that of a ship's foghorn on a mist-filled night. The room shook with the sound of it. Cracks crawled down the walls, chunks of drywall falling to the floor, revealing more of that cold, blue light. The room was filled with light now, as if there were no ceiling and it was a snowy January day. Liam shivered.

He lifted the book closer to his face. Then he squeezed his eyes shut. *Believe, believe, believe.* He closed his eyes, squeezing them shut so hard that his eyeballs ached. He knew a prayer, knew it because it was burned into his memory. It was the prayer that his mother had muttered on her deathbed, over and over again as she beseeched God to look out for him and keep watch over him. He said this prayer now, his lips mumbling over the words. *Believe, believe, believe.* He tore through his defenses, his own logic. He had seen enough to know that God was not a figment of the imagination. He had seen enough to know that the creature upon the bed was not a manifestation of an altered reality. He had seen and felt God's presence in the room. He fought himself, his logic, his education, and he let himself believe. He opened himself to faith, to things he had not believed in since he was a boy. As if he had opened up a sluice gate, something filled his body, making him tremble and gasp for breath. But it wasn't pain he felt. It was something else, something indescribable, a comfort, a power. He felt insignificant, but gloriously so. It made no sense to him, but Liam let that power wash through him, didn't deny it, didn't fight it. He just let it be. When he opened his eyes, he saw the room through a golden light. The blue-light of the creature on the bed was still there, but he knew, the golden light would win out in the end.

"Ok. I'm ready," he said. He raised the aspergillum into the air and brought his arm down once again. The water splashed across Maddie's skin, sizzling upon contact, and Maddie howled in pain. It was barely noticeable, but he thought he saw the blue-light in the room dim slightly.

"I banish you, demon. In the Lord's name. I banish you." He splashed her with more holy water, and Maddie screamed and thrashed on the bed some more. He spoke now without the book in his hand, and he understood that the book was a starting point, a way to link to the power that was needed. The words did not matter so much as the intent; this is what the power inside him communicated, not in sound, or in thought, but in pure feeling. Every cell in his body listened to something outside of himself, something greater. Golden light filled the room, choking out the blue. "This plane is not for you. You had your time. Now it is the Lord's time. I banish you, demon. I banish you back to Hell."

Maddie shrieked, and Scott and Angela writhed next to Liam as they tried to maintain their grip upon Maddie's feet. The child's body rose up off the bed, hanging in the air, her bonds stretching tight as the creature inside sought any way to escape. Her body vibrated with that pulsing blue light, as the golden light surrounded her.

"Tell me your name, demon!"

"Never!" Maddie moaned.

Liam splashed Maddie with more holy water, yelling, "Tell me your name!"

"My name is sin!" Maddie shouted, the creature inside still fighting.

The entire bed lifted off the ground now, moving further and further upward. Liam splashed the creature with more holy water, as Scott and Angela struggled to keep the bed from floating too high.

"Hold her down!" Scott yelled to Angela. "If she gets too high, we'll lose touch." Angela grunted and groaned as she tried to pull the bed down with her free hand while still maintaining contact with Maddie's foot.

"Excellent," Father Romero said to Liam. "I can feel his presence filling the room. Keep pressing, Liam."

Liam looked skyward, squeezing his eyes shut. He couldn't see it, but the presence filling his body let him know everything, let him know that the bed was floating higher and higher, and that Angela, shorter than Scott was about to lose touch with Maddie's ankle. Even with his eyes closed, he could see her struggling to maintain her grip.

"It's getting too high!" Angela wailed. "I'm going to lose it."

There was a thump as Father Romero leaped onto the bed, diving on top of Maddie and forcing the bed to crash back down to the ground.

It is time. Liam opened his eyes, and the world was awash with things he could not understand. It was as if he could see everything, every molecule in the room. On the bed, darkness thrashed inside Maddie, a wavering black cloud. He pointed at the creature on the bed, hiding inside the little girl, and opened his mouth. Words came out, words he didn't know, words he couldn't even recall as soon as he was done saying them. They were not his words; they were the words of something greater than him.

The black cloud vibrated, and Maddie opened her mouth and screamed in pain.

"Tell me your name!" Liam bellowed.

Maddie thrashed on the bed, wrists and ankles bleeding profusely, soiling the white sheets underneath. "Kosholap!" Maddie wailed, her voice filled with equal measures of pain, sorrow, and rage. "My name is Kosholap!"

He had it now. The name. The key. The bargain would be fulfilled, the world restored to order. "By the divine wrath of God, I expel thee from this mortal vessel and into the pit of darkness for all of eternity. Kosholap..." At the sound of its name, Maddie screamed, shrieking, its voice carrying the hint of an eternity of torture. His words trailed off... there was no more need for them... there was only need of the name now.

The bed lifted skyward, forcing Angela and Scott to lose their grip. It rolled over slowly, and Father Romero slid off and to the ground with a thump. Once the bed was upside down, it stopped turning. The legs of the bed thumped into the ceiling. It began to turn clockwise, rotating above. Maddie's skin began to blacken, as if being charred by flames. Her skin began to crack, faintly.

"Kosholap," Liam said.

The cracks raced across Maddie's body like lightning bolts. In the spaces between the cracks, there was no longer blue light, but golden light, the light of the morning sun. Maddie hung from the bed, still bound by rope, violently thrashing about, defying gravity.

"Kosholap!" Liam shouted.

The cracks grew wider, the light brighter until none but Liam could bear to look at it. Liam moved directly underneath the bed, putting his face nose to nose with the suspended form of Maddie. He pointed up at her, golden light filling his hands.

The room seemed to still for a second as if in anticipation. The wind stopped blowing. The curtains fell slowly to their resting position. Maddie stopped bellowing and stared at Liam, a faint hint of the blue light still in her eyes. Everyone in the room held their breath.

"Kosholap," Liam said in a whisper. Maddie's body filled with the golden light, the light of God. The room brightened until it felt as if they were standing in the noon sun of an August afternoon. A thunderclap shook the room, followed by an explosion. Everyone who had been standing found themselves on the floor, their heads ringing. Liam fell straight down onto the floor, looking up at the levitating bed above him.

The cracked, black skin exploded from Maddie's body, propelled outward by an unseen force. The skin withered away like airborne bits of burning newspaper. On the ground, bits of the skin covered Liam's face, and he breathed them in. He began to choke immediately.

For a brief second, Maddie hung suspended in the air, and then Maddie and the bed crashed down onto Liam.

****

The room was quiet, and then Angela and Scott scrambled to their feet. They worked to flip the bed over. Its metal frame seemed to weigh a thousand pounds. They saw Maddie still lying on the bed, unconscious, her hands and feet still bound to the metal railings. Angela and Scott were too busy untying Maddie's wrists and ankles to notice the small puff of smoke that escaped from Liam's lips.

"What's happening? Is she alright?" Father Romero asked.

Scott and Angela finally finished untying Maddie, and they looked her over. The wounds of the night were nowhere to be seen. Even her wrists and ankles, bound for so long, showed no sign of damage. Looking at Maddie on the bed, sleeping, her hair looking healthier than it had in months, Angela couldn't believe it.

"Maddie?" Scott asked, grabbing one of her hands and squeezing it.

Angela grabbed the other. Her daughter's hand was warm and soft. "Maddie? Can you hear us?" she asked gently.

Slowly, Maddie's eyes opened. She blinked and blinked, until her eyes would focus, and then she saw them, holding her hands in theirs. "Mom? Dad?"

Scott and Angela breathed a sigh of relief, and they pulled Maddie to a sitting position and wrapped their arms around her. *She's alive. She's alive, and she's perfect,* Angela thought. Tears sprang to her eyes to match the one's she saw running down Scott's cheeks.

From the floor, they heard a voice. "Is Liam alright?" Father Romero asked. Father Romero struggled to his feet, his hands held out before him.

Oh, my God, Liam. She felt terrible for having forgotten about him. They had been so worried about Maddie, that they hadn't even stopped to check on him. The electric bed must have weighed a good five-hundred pounds.

Scott unwrapped his arms from Maddie and squatted down over the body of Liam. "Liam?" he asked, gently slapping Liam's face to waken him. He had to repeat his name several times, but finally, Liam opened his eyes.

"I'm awake," he said, his voice cold, emotionless.

No one noticed Father Romero's jaw clench. If he had still had eyes, they would have showed his concern.

Epilogue

Maddie sat in the doctor's office surrounded by her family. Her little brother played with an office toy, one of those wire and wooden bead thingies. He happily pushed the beads this way and that, and she smiled. She remembered how much she had loved that thing when she was a kid. It seemed to her mind that the toy only existed in doctors' offices, as she had never seen one anywhere else.

Her mother and father sat close to her, her mom lightly stroking her arm and her dad holding her hand. Ever since she had woken up two weeks ago, they hadn't left her alone. Truth be told, she didn't want them to. When she had awoken to find them there, it was as if a lifetime had passed since she had seen them. Her memory was still spotty, and Maddie found the story they had told hard to believe. But she had seen the wounds on her parents and Father Romero. An image of Father Romero's eyeless face flashed in her mind, and she tried not to think about her fingers gouging out his eyes.

Liam, her savior, sat next to them. She found him odd as a person, but he had saved her life, so she showed him gratitude as she should. But still, there was something about him that was familiar. She couldn't quite put her finger on it. As she was trying to puzzle it out, Dr. Wong stepped out from the door that led back to the medical rooms.

They stood to follow her back to her office, but she didn't even let them move before she pronounced, "This is simply amazing."

"What?" Maddie asked.

Dr. Wong flicked a glance at a chart in her hands, as if she still couldn't believe it, and then she dropped it to her side. "I've never seen anything like this before?"

"What is it?" Angela asked, an edge of worry to her voice.

"It's as if Maddie never had cancer at all. There's no trace of it. In fact, she's healthier than ever."

No cancer. Maddie had dreamed of those words for so long, to actually hear them said out loud, by her doctor no less... well, it was all too unreal. Her mother and father hugged her tight. They didn't notice Liam sitting in a lobby chair, stone-faced, the news meaning as much to him as the fact that the sun had come up that morning.

****

Outside the hospital, Scott watched as his family headed to the parking lot. But Scott stayed behind to talk to Liam. He had never gotten around to properly thanking the man, and he figured now was as good a time as any. With his cure confirmed, who knew how busy he would be trying to convince other doctors of the cure?

"Thank you," Scott said, holding his hand out.

Liam looked down at his hand as if it were an alien thing. Then he reached out and shook it.

"So what are you going to do now?" Scott asked.

"I don't know," Liam said. "The cure is too risky. I guess I'll just continue my studies."

Scott frowned a bit. It seemed a little out of character for the boy. He had been so fervent, so driven before Maddie had returned... before the night that he had saved his daughter. "But don't you think people should know?" he asked.

"Maybe when I'm actually a doctor, I'll try again," Liam said.

That made sense. He would be in some serious trouble if people found out he had been pretending to be a doctor. Scott would never tell. He owed the boy that much. "Well, if you ever need anything, just let me know. There's no way that I can ever repay you." He meant it. Though Liam was bizarre, anti-social, and perhaps too curious for his own good, there was nothing he could deny him for saving the life of his daughter.

"I'll let you know," Liam said.

Scott moved to walk to the parking garage, but then he stopped. "Do you want a ride?" he asked looking over his shoulder at Liam. "It looks like it's going to rain."

"No, thank you. I'm going to stop by and pay a visit to Father Romero," Liam said.

Scott shrugged his shoulders. "Suit yourself. Tell him we said hello, and we'll stop by on Friday."

"I will," Liam said.

Scott turned and left Liam standing in front of the hospital. As soon as he made it under the cover of the parking garage, the sky began to dump rain. Scott looked over his shoulder once to see Liam standing in the rain, his face cold and impassive. *Such an odd duck,* he thought.

****

Father Romero lay in his bed, trying not to think about the pain of his ruined eye sockets. He tried not to think about a lot of things if he was being truly honest. He tried not to think of his lost eyesight. He tried not to think of the implications of Maddie's miraculous recovery. He tried not to think about the damage that had been done to the souls of the Cutters. Most of all, he tried not to think about the price...

He sensed a presence in his room. Even without eyes, he could tell that someone was there, and he had a suspicion of who it would be. "I knew you'd come for me," he said.

He sensed the smile in the being's words as he spoke. "You didn't tell them who I really am? What I am?" the being asked using Liam's voice.

Informing the Cutters about Liam was the last thing he would ever do. "There was no need. They have what they desire now. Let them enjoy their happiness."

"Are you ready?" the being asked him.

Father Romero thought about the price then. He thought about what he had learned in school. A demon could not be banished. A demon could only be displaced. The only way to truly get rid of a demon was to kill the flesh that it inhabited, which was why he had volunteered to do the exorcism in the first place. Let it inhabit him, and he would do the rest himself. It was one of the reasons exorcisms were so rare. Few priests, knowing the consequences of an exorcism, would let a demon infest their own bodies.

He had almost told Liam of the consequences, but he suspected the boy wouldn't have gone through with the ritual. It was the price of saving that girl. He hoped Maddie would never know how much her life had cost... three lives, his, Matt's, and Liam's, so that the Cutters might foil God's plans. He hoped she made that life worth it. He hoped she went on to do great things. "If it's my time, then it is God's will," he said.

The being at the foot of his bed smiled, a blue light flashing deep in his eyes. He walked towards Father Romero's bed. "Oh, it's your time, but it's my will."

Father Romero's screams echoed through the hospital.

A Word From Jacy

Thank you for reading An Unorthodox Cure. If you've made it this far, I'm guessing you enjoyed the ride. Please leave a review! As an indie author, the only marketing I receive is from fellow readers like you!

If you enjoyed An Unorthodox Cure, you might enjoy my apocalyptic series, This Rotten World, a sprawling zombie apocalypse tale that will drag you kicking and screaming to the end of the world. It's my most popular series of novels. They are available to buy and also free as part of your Kindle Unlimited subscription.

I am currently working on the final chapter of This Rotten World, and it should be available on amazon by the end of 2020.

What are you waiting for? The zombie apocalypse is just starting – and no one knows who will survive and who will join the ranks of the living dead.

Get Free Stuff from Jacy Morris

Building a relationship with my readers is super important to me. Please join my newsletter for information on new books and deals plus all this free content:

1. A free copy of This Rotten World: Part One.

2. A free copy of The City That Never Was, a horror novella inspired by real life.

3. A free copy of The Pied Piper of Hamelin, a twisted fairy tale like nothing you've ever seen before.

You can get your content for free, by signing up at jacymorris.com

Also By Jacy Morris

In the This Rotten World Series

This Rotten World

A sickness runs rampant through the world. In Portland, Oregon it is no different. As the night takes hold, eight men and women bear witness to the horror of a zombie outbreak. This Rotten World is the zombie novel that horror fans have been waiting for. Where other zombie works skip over the best part of a zombie outbreak, This Rotten World revels in it the downfall of humanity, dragging you through the beginnings of society's death, kicking and screaming.

Available on Amazon

This Rotten World: Let It Burn

It didn't take long for Portland, Oregon to fall. Amid a decaying and crumbling city, a group of survivors hides amid the smoke and the fire. They need to get out of the city... which is easier said than done with thousands of zombies blocking the path. Witness the terrifying flight of these survivors as they leave the city behind and Let It Burn.

Available on Amazon

This Rotten World: No More Heroes

With the smoking ruins of Portland behind them, our survivors find that they have a new enemy to contend with... other survivors. With the dead hounding them at every step and humanity struggling to hold onto its civility, the survivors face their greatest challenge yet. At the end of this battle, there will be No More Heroes.

Available on Amazon

In the Enemies of Our Ancestors Series

The Enemies of Our Ancestors

In the mountains of the Southwest, in the time before the continents were known, the future of the entire world rested upon the shoulders of a boy prophet whose abduction would threaten to break the world. As a youth, Kochen witnessed the death of his father at the hands of a gruesome spirit that stalked his village's farmlands. From that moment forth, he became a ward of the priests of the village in the cliffs. As he grew, he would begin to experience horrific visions, gifts from the spirits, that all of the other priests dismissed. When the ancient enemies of the Cliff People raid the village and steal Kochen away, they set in motion world-changing events, which threaten to break the shackles that bind the spirits to the earth. A group of hunters are sent to bring Kochen back to his rightful place. As Kochen's power grows, so too does the power of the spirits, and with the help of an ancient seer and his hunter allies, he seeks to restore balance to the world as it falls into brutal madness.

Available on Amazon

The Enemies of Our Ancestors: The Cult of the Skull

With the world balanced after the tragedies of the year before, two tribes attempt to come together and form a whole. But as an ancient foe from the past reappears and a new threat from the south snakes its way to them, the Stick

People and the Cliff People must do more than put their differences aside... they must come together to survive. As fantastic as it is violent, The Cult of the Skull picks up right where The Enemies of Our Ancestors left off.

Available on Amazon

Standalone Novels

The Abbey

In the desolate mountains of Scotland, there is an abbey that time has forgotten. Its buildings have crumbled, and the monks that once lived there, guarding the abbey's secret, are long dead. When the journal of a crazed monk is discovered, so is the secret of Inchorgrath Abbey. There are tunnels underneath the abbey and in them resides a secret long forgotten. Together with a group of mercenaries, her would-be boyfriend, and her cutthroat professor, Lasha Arkeketa will travel across the world to uncover the secret of The Abbey.

Available on Amazon

The Pied Piper of Hamelin

A sickness has come to the village of Hamelin. Born on the backs of rats, a plague begins to spread. As the town rips itself apart, a stranger appears to offer them salvation. But when the citizens of the town fail to hold up their end of the bargain, the stranger returns and exacts a toll that is still spoken of to this day. That toll? The town's entire population of children. This is the legend of the Pied Piper. It is no fairy tale. It is a nightmare. Are you prepared to hear his song?

Available on Amazon

Killing the Cult

At any one time, there are 4,000 cults operating within the United States. In Logansport, Indiana, one cult is growing. When The Benevolent recruit Matt Rust's estranged daughter, he journeys to their compound to free her, one way or another. Unfortunately, for Matt Rust, his checkered past threatens to derail his rescue mission. When word gets out that Rust has reemerged after spending the last decade in the witness protection program, drug tzar Emilio Cartagena sends his best men after Rust. Will he be able to save his daughter before Cartagena's men arrive? Find out as Matt Rust tries Killing the Cult.

Available on Amazon

The Lady That Stayed

Land has a price. It's always been that way. When J.S. Stensrud and his wife Dotty buy a piece of land on the Oregon coast known as the Spit, they come to know that price. As Stensrud tries to build a legacy on his island amid the background of the Great Depression, he is visited by a Native American woman who helps him learn the bloody price of land in the most painful way possible.

Available on Amazon

The Drop

How many hearts can a song touch? How many ears can it reach? How many people can it kill? When popular boy band Whoa-Town releases their latest album, no one thinks anything of it. They certainly don't think that the world will be changed forever. After an apocalyptic disease sweeps the world, it becomes clear that the music of this seemingly innocuous boy band had something to do with it, but how? Katherine Maddox, her life irrevocably changed by a disease dubbed The Drop, sets out to find out how and why, to prevent something like The Drop from ever happening again.

About the Author

Jacy Morris is a Native American author who has brought to life zombies, cults, demons, and spirits. You can learn more about him at the following:

http://jacymorris.com

jacy@jacymorris.com

Be sure to check out

The Abbey

By Jacy Morris

Here is a sneak preview:

THE ABBEY

PROLOGUE

He would make him scream. So far they had all screamed, their unused voices quaking and cracking with pain that was made even worse by the fact that they were breaking their vows to their Lord, their sole reason for existence. Shattering their vows was their last act on earth, and then they were gone. Now there was only one left. A lone monk had taken flight into the abbey's lower regions, a labyrinthine winding of corridors and catacombs lined with the boxed up remains of the dead and their trinkets.

Brenley Denman's boots clanked off of the rough-hewn, blue stone as he trounced through the abbey's crypts, following the whiff of smoke from the monk's torch and the echo of his harried footsteps. His men were spread out through the underworks, funneling the monk ahead of them, driving him the way hounds drove a fox. The monk would lead them to his den, and then the prize would be theirs. And then the world.

He held his torch up high, watching the flames glimmer off of golden urns and silver swords, ancient relics of a nobility that had long since gone extinct, their glory only known by faded etchings in marble sarcophagi, the remaining glint of their once-prized possessions, and the spiders who built their webs in the darkness. Once they were done with the monk, they would take anything that glittered, but first they needed the talisman, the fabled bauble that resided at the bottom of the mountain the abbey was built on.

Throughout the land, legends of the talisman had been told for decades around hearthfires and inns throughout the isles. Then the tellers had begun to vanish, until the talisman of Inchorgrath and its stories had all but been forgotten. But Denman knew. He remembered the stories his father had told him while they sat around the fire of their stone house, built less than ten yards from the cemetery. His father's knuckles were cracked and dried from hours in the elements digging graves and rifling pockets when no one was looking. He knew secrets when he saw them. His father had first heard the story from the old Celts, the remains of the land's indigenous population, reduced to poverty and begging in the streets. His father said the old Celts' stories were two-thirds bullshit and one-third truth. They told of a relic, a key to the Celts' uprising and reclamation of the land, buried in the deepest part of the tallest mountain on the Isles. Of course, they spoke of regeneration and the return of Gods among men as well, but the relic... that was the important part. That was the part that was worth money. And now, he was here, with his men, ready to make his fortune.

He heard shouts, but it was impossible to tell where they were coming from. Sound echoed and bounced off of the blue, quartzite stone blocks, warping reality. He chose the corridor to his right, quickening his pace, his long legs eating up the distance. His men knew not to start without him, but you never knew when a monk would lash out, going against their discipline and training and earning a sword through the throat for their duplicity. That would be unacceptable to Denman. The monk must scream before he died.

His breathing quickened along with his pace, and he could feel the warmth of anticipation spread through his limbs as his breath puffed into the cold crypt air. Miles... they had come miles through these crypts, twisting and turning, burrowing into the secret heart of the earth, chasing the last monk who skittered through the hallways like a spider. The other monks had all known the secret of the abbey, the power it harbored, the relic it hid in its bowels. To a man, they had sat on their knees, their robes collecting condensation in the green grass of the morning, refusing to divulge the abbey's mysteries.

They had died, twisted, mangled and beaten. But still, all he could pull from them were the screams, musical expulsions of the throat that he ended with a smile as he dragged the razor-fine edge of his knife across their throats. Their blood had bubbled out, vivid against the morning sun, to splash on the grass.

When there was only one left, they had let him go. The youngest monk in the abbey, grown to manhood, but still soft about the face, his intelligent eyes filled with horror, stood and ran, his robe stained with the pooled blood of the monks that had died to his left and right. He was like one of the homing pigeons they used in the lowlands, leading them to home... to the relic. They had chased him, hooting and hollering the whole way, their voices and taunts driving the monk before them like a fox. The chase would end at his burrow; it always did.

Ahead, he heard laughing, and with that Denman knew that the chase was at an end. He rounded one last corner to see the monk being worked over by his men, savage pieces of stupidity who were good for two things, lifting heavy objects and killing people. Denman waved his hand and they let the suffering monk go. The monk sagged to the ground, his head bent over, his eyes leaking tears. He sobbed in silence.

Denman stood in the secret of the crypt, a room at the heart of the mountain, the place where legends hid. How deep had they gone? At first there had been stairs, but then they had reached a deeper part of the crypt where the corridors twisted and turned, the floor pitched ever downward. Time and distance had lost all meaning in the breast of the world. How long had it taken them to carve this place, the monks working in silence to protect their treasure? Hundreds of years? A thousand?

The room was simple and small, as the order's aesthetics demanded, filled by Denman and the nine men that he had brought to take the abbey's secrets. Wait, one was missing. He looked at his men, brutal pieces of humanity, covered in dirt, mud and blood. The boy wasn't there. Denman shrugged. He would find his way down eventually.

The walls of the room were blue-gray, stone blocks stacked one on top of the other without the benefit of mortar, the weight of the mountain providing the only glue that was needed. The only other features of the room were an alcove with two thick, tallow candles in cheap tin holders and an ancient oak table.

The smoke from his men's torches hung in the air, creating a stinging miasma that stung his eyes. Brenley Denman squatted next to the monk and used his weathered hand to raise the monk's head by his chin. He looked into the monk's eyes, and instead of the fear that he expected to see, there was something else.

"What is this? Defiance?" he asked, amused by the monk's bravado. Denman stood and kicked the monk in the mouth with his boot, a shit-covered piece of leather that was harder than his heart; teeth and blood decorated the stones.

"Where is it?" he asked the monk. There was no answer. Denman had expected none. Say what you will about the Lord's terrestrial servants, but they were loyal... which made everything more difficult... more exhilarating. Denman was a man that loved a challenge.

He handed his torch to one of his men, a broken-faced simpleton whose only gifts were strength and the ability to do what he was told. Denman knew that he would need both hands to make the monk sing his secrets.

"Hand me the Tearmaker," he said to another of his men. Radan, built like a rat with stubby arms and powerful legs, reached to his belt and produced a knife, skinny and flexible, designed not so much for murder as it was for removing savory meat from skin and fat. It made excellent work of fish, and it would most likely prove delightfully deft at making a tight-lipped monk break his vows.

As he reached out to take the proffered knife from his man, the monk scrambled to his feet and dove for the alcove. Before they could stop him, the monk grasped both of the candle sticks and yanked on them. The candlesticks rose into the air. Rusted, metal chains were affixed to their bases, and they clanked against the surrounding stone of the alcove as the monk pulled on them.

The distant sound of stones grinding upon stones reverberated throughout the crypt. Somewhere, something was moving. Denman glared at the monk. The robed figure dropped the candlesticks and turned to face them. With his head cast downward, he reached into the folds of his robe and produced a rosary. He folded his hands and began to pray, beads moving through his fingers, his lips moving without making sound.

The crypt shook as an unseen weight clattered through the halls of the crypt. Dust fell from the ceiling, hanging in the air, buoyed upwards by the tumbling smoke of their torches.

"What have you done?" Denman asked.

The monk did not respond. Instead, he reached into the hanging sleeve of one of his robes and produced a small stone thimble, roughly-made and ancient. It was shiny and black, the type of black that seemed to steal the light from the room. The monk put it up to his mouth, hesitated for a second and then swallowed it, grimacing in pain as the object slid down his throat.

In the hallway behind them, the grinding had stopped. The crypt was silent, but for the guttering of the torches and their own breathing. "Go see what happened," he said to the oaf and the rat. The other men followed them, leaving Denman alone with the monk and his unceasing, silent supplications to the Lord above.

Denman forced the monk onto the oak table. He offered little resistance. With Tearmaker in his hand, Denman began to carve the skin lovingly off of the monk's fingers. First, he carved a circle around the man's fingers, then a line. With the edge of his knife, he prodded a corner of the skin up, and then, grasping tightly, he ripped the skin away from the muscle and bone, dropping the wet flesh onto the ground. He did this to each finger, one by one. Sweat stood out on Denman's brow, and the monk had yet to scream. He hadn't so much as gasped or hissed in pain. He was turning out to be more work than he was worth. Except for the blood pulsing from his skinned fingers, he appeared to be asleep, his eyes softly closed.

"Where is it, you bastard?" There was no response but for the bleeding.

Denman pulled the monk's robe up around his waist. It was a quick jump, but he was eager to be done with the man on the table. Usually, he would take his time with a challenge like the monk, savoring the sensation of skin ripping from muscle and bone, but he could feel the weight of the mountain about him, its walls shrinking with every minute. Sweat covered his body, and the monk's calm demeanor was unnerving.

Radan rounded the corner at a run, his body dripping with sweat and panic on his face. He skidded to a stop, his boots grinding dust into the blue stones. "We're sealed in here," he said.

Denman looked at the monk lying on the table. His hand gripped Tearmaker tight. "What have you done?" The monk lay there, his eyes closed, a look of peace on his face. "What have you done!" he screamed, jabbing the knife into the monk's ribs. Then Denman saw the monk's hands.

Where before his index and pointer finger had been reduced to skinless chunks of muscle and bone dripping blood on the table, there was now skin. "Impossible," Denman whispered.

The monk's eyes snapped open, and finally, Denman got the scream that he had been waiting for.

Be sure to check out

THE PIED PIPER OF HAMELIN

By Jacy Morris

Here is a sneak preview:

The Pied Piper of Hamelin

Prologue: The River Weser

The boat captain sailed down the river, the wind ruffling his long, salt-and-pepper locks. It was a fine day. His ship was laden with goods, and he was relishing the prospect of turning a nice profit for himself and his crew. He should have been happy, ecstatic, singing shanties that would turn a barmaid's face red, but he wasn't.

The captain sniffed inward, pulling a grimy film of mucus into the back of his throat. He hacked up a thick glob and deposited it into the Weser River. He could taste the blood in it. His men were no better. Though they were ill, they still did their jobs. After all, a boatswain who couldn't earn his keep wouldn't receive his full share. On top of that, as an example to his men, the captain continued to work, stalking the decks and shouting out orders, though all he wanted to do was go down below and curl up in his cabin. He felt as if his head was trying to split in half, and he had an uncomfortable swelling in his groin that sent sharp pains through his entire body every time he moved.

Out of the corner of his eye, he spied furtive movement. Goddamn rats, he thought to himself. He would have to see if he could find some sort of boat cat in the next town. He consulted his charts, hand-drawn, passed down from captain to captain, and saw that the next village would be Hamelin.

It was an uppity berg; the mayor was trying to turn it into Rome from what the goodfolk at the pier told him. They had no need of Rome in this part of the world. What they needed was good strong ale, women with weak morals, and more good strong ale. Or maybe that's just what he needed.

A chilly breeze washed over the river, and the captain pulled his jacket tighter, gritting his teeth at the sharp pain the movement caused him. Underneath his arms, there were more swellings, unnatural lumps that seemed as if they were nothing but bundles of nerves. Pulling the jacket tighter had been like jabbing a flame-heated knife, point first, into each of his armpits.

Without warning, he began to cough like he had never coughed before. Black spots swam in front of his eyes, and for a brief moment, he thought, *This is it. This is how I die.* But then the coughing passed, and he was able to grab a raspy breath of air. The muscles in his back felt worse for wear, and he spat a wad of red-flecked phlegm into the river.

The breeze kicked up again, but this time, he didn't bother to readjust his jacket. Instead, he let the wind wash over him, evaporating the fever sweat from his brow.

"Captain," his first mate said, "Old Gert is dead."

It took a while for the words to sink into his fever-addled mind, but when they did, he did the only thing he could do. "Pitch him over the side, lad. It's a water-burial for him."

Normally, they would keep the body in the cold hull of the ship so that his family could bury him proper, but with all of the rats on board, it would be more dignified to give him to the river than to let those furry bastards make a meal out of him.

The first mate scuttled off to do his bidding without question. That was good. It meant that the crew didn't think he was responsible for the plague that had descended upon them. Sailors were a superstitious lot, but the captain had never held stock with the ridiculous notions of superstition. But that didn't mean that his crew wouldn't turn on him if more started to die.

He heard the sound of scurrying across the deck. "What the hell was that?" he wondered aloud. Spinning around quickly, he caught sight of movement out of the corner of his eye. It was another rat, a huge one. He chased it across the deck for a few steps, but then stopped due to the pain. After the first couple of steps, the lumps in his groin shot fire through his entire body. He vowed to find a cat when they got to Hamelin. In the meantime, he said a prayer for Old Gert as his body splashed into the river.

The rats watched and listened, the fleas on their backs oblivious to everything but the flesh in front of them and the blood underneath.

Be sure to check out

THE DROP

By Jacy Morris

Here is a sneak preview:

PROLOGUE

An excerpt from an article entitled "Whoa-Town Becoming Whoa-World in Record Time" by Anton Russo as Published in *Rolling Stone*

Part of me wants to hate them. Boy bands aren't supposed to be this good. A man, a grown-ass, thirty-year-old man, shouldn't find himself moved by the vocal-stylings of five boys, some not even old enough to drink yet. But here I am, at Wembley Stadium, packed in like cattle in a slaughterhouse chute, ready to stick my head into the kill box and have a hole punched in my cranium.

There is no opening band for Whoa-Town. What sucker would take that gig? Who would want to have the memory of their performance obliterated by the next act, a band that many claim is bigger than the Beatles and the Stones combined? Lofty words. All of us scoffing, bearded, music snobs sneer, knowing full well in our hearts that there is no way anyone means it when they throw out those comparisons. It's just the thing that clichéd, hack journalists say when they can't think of any way of telling people how big a band is or is going to be.

Here I am, standing amid the heat and the hot breath of 90,000 people, the lucky ones who snagged their tickets in that first two minutes before the entire system crashed. Leading to a day in London collectively known as Cry Day, the day that every teenage girl, and many other men, women, and boys christened their cell phones with tears at news that the Whoa-Town show was already sold out.

You'd expect the air to reek of cheap designer-knockoff perfume, hair product and bubblegum. But it doesn't. It smells of something else. It reeks instead of lust and anticipation. The crowd hums with energy; their faces drip sweat even though the stadium's roof is open to the elements. The cool night air can't compete with their fever. Their bodies vibrate, conducting heat at a level that confirms in my mind that spontaneous combustion might actually be a thing. At any moment, the girl next to me, screaming ear-piercing "woos" every thirty seconds or so, might burst into flames.

Before long, we can't take it anymore. Wait... they can't take it. I'm certainly not into any boy band. I'm just here for the story. They begin to chant. When the mother next to me, clad in baggy jeans that go up past her bellybutton, elbows me as encouragement, I make a show of reluctantly joining in. I clap. I yell, "Whoa-Town!" right along with everyone else.

Only when the building quakes from all the stomping, yelling, and clapping does something happen. Just as I am assured that Wembley Stadium will collapse around us before the band ever takes stage, the lights come on, blinding us. The lights fade, dropping faster than my own aloof persona, plunging us into a darkness punctuated by the unwelcome glow of emergency lighting. Around the stadium, tiny rectangular blooms of blue-light illuminate in response. 90,000 people recording when they aren't supposed to be. It is as if the stadium is filled with thousands of mutant fireflies, swaying from side to side as the chant of "Whoa-Town!" thunders through the stadium once again... and then the beat drops.

With a "whoomp," several sparking shapes arc into the air, erupting into gold and crimson starbursts, and screams echo so loudly that I'm not even sure when the screaming stops and the music begins. They're here. Whoa-Town, the boys that will change music and the world forever and I, Anton Russo, was there.

Tragic. Just tragic. - Sebastian

You think that's tragic, check out those *Teen Beat* articles I found. - Katherine

Chapter 1: Walking the Streets

I see this story as more than a job, more than just a fact-finding mission to once again help us cope with the tragedy, with a loss that, in a very real sense, is unprecedented. Many people have tried that. So many. No, if that's all this was, then I would be off somewhere else, looking into a murder or trying to uncover the next dastardly person exploiting the American Relief Organization.

I see this story as a time capsule, a way to help the people of the future. If there's one thing that I learned from my 8th-grade social studies teacher, it's that history is a cycle, and that all things, good or bad, will come around again, hence the term revolution, a circuit, a never-ending loop that only the educated can see. Thinking about what the world has just gone through, and is still going through, I can only shudder at the thought that hundreds of years down the line this will all happen again. So my hope is to write this story, bury it in the ground, and when it's needed, the people of the future can come and dig it up.

People will need to know, not so much the people that are still alive, but the people of the future. The people still alive already know about The Drop. They're so tired of thinking about it that they don't actually want to know the truth of the situation. They can't help but see The Drop around them. Examining it further is just poking at a poorly stitched together wound with a razorblade. Sooner or later it's going to open up. Sooner or later, it's going to bleed. They don't want to know how the knife that stabbed them in the chest was forged. They don't want to know where the steel came from, how the ivory handle was carved from the tusk of a poached elephant. None of that will help them. But for the people of the future, that's a different story altogether. The Drop was our Black Plague, and just as our knowledge of the spread of the plague prevents it from happening again, this article is vital to preventing another Drop.

I'm in the Big Apple. They call it the Big Rotten Core now. As I walk down Broadway, I'm struck by its similarity to the post-apocalyptic movies I over-consumed as a teenager. The emptiness of the streets, very *I Am Legend.* The newspaper tumbling through the intersection, unchecked like a tumbleweed through a western town, very *The Road.* The sad motherfucker leaning up against the wall, smoking a cigarette, and staring at the cracked and crumbling concrete, very *Book of Eli.*

The street ends at Times Square, once a mega-hub of awesomeness where cowboys played guitar in their underwear and an unceasing cavalcade of electric, sex-themed ads assaulted wayward tourists. It was now just a scene from *The Postman*. There weren't enough people to provide upkeep for the cities. Those that stayed did so because they had become ghosts themselves, haunted by the losses of The Drop. They stuck around, though no more food was coming, except for that which they grew themselves. Though the children didn't play hopscotch on the streets and the stoplights had been turned off, the ghosts remained, remembering the glory of New York and its eight-and-a-half-million residents.

Glass crunches under my boots as I turn and look inside the Disney Store... all those toys just sitting there, no one left to play with them. I step inside. The cash register was busted open a long time ago, but the toys sit waiting. And I can't help but wonder who will actually benefit from the story that I am going to tell.

The next generation, I suppose, the ones that will grow up without music. The ones that will grow up without the internet, they'll want these dolls. They'll want something to play with.

I exit the Disney Store, sick of looking at clownish, Dory plush dolls. I am in time for the show. The man at the end of the street puts a gun in his mouth and pulls the trigger. Blood sprays the wall behind him. I scream like a maniac, but somehow, no one in Times Square hears me... because I'm the only person left alive in a place that was once called "The Crossroads of the World." And I wonder, was that man just waiting for someone to stumble along? Was he waiting for an audience before he killed himself? Or were his sixty days up?

I shudder and call the police. "Hello?... Yeah, there's been a suicide in Times Square... What do you mean three hours?"

I hang up. I go back inside the Disney store, and I grab myself a Dory plushy, and I hold onto it for dear life as the man's blood and brains run down the wall. This was probably the worst vacation idea I had ever had.